BEYON

Book One

A series of post-human short stories and images

By

Angel Martin

Artwork by Angel Martin - Cyber Studio's

To my Princess.
My soulmate, my friend and companion.
Thank you for always being there for me.

CONTENTS

Amrita Ram was the CEO of one of the most powerful corporations the world had ever seen.

Time magazine described her as 'The New Messiah', a slightly tongue-in-cheek reference to the simple fact that there was barely a person on the planet that didn't have a device, medication or software that didn't have a Ram patent. Her subsequent disappearance created a media frenzy, whose speculation was only quelled when her body parts were fished out of the waters off the coast of Rio de Janeiro. This however was not the last the world would hear of Amrita, her legacy would haunt humanity for eternity.

The year is 2147. Ryan is a detective in the London police department, he is at the end of a forty year career where he has seen technology completely change the nature of policing. He feels like a dinosaur in this ultra-modern world and he counts the days to his retirement. The police department is now privately run and with the exception of the senior staff, androids have replaced the rank and file. Cybercrime is on the rise but serious street crime for the most part has been eradicated, making the current series of murders particularly puzzling. Ryan and his android partner will have to learn to work together if they are to solve the Ripper case.

In 1984 the SAS stormed the Libyan embassy in a very

public display to clearly illustrate that the United Kingdom did not negotiate with terrorists. Forty years on we are gripped by an escalating scale of terrorist threats using the world's press to broadcast its atrocities. The Ministry of Defence has decided it's time to push back, to reinvent the nature of urban combat using the latest technology and take the fight to them. To fight fire with fire. This is the story of Andrew McCabe, who was instrumental in that fight.

An off-world mining colony received an automated distress signal from the *USSR Kepler*, an exploration vessel that had been lost in space for over two hundred years. The salvage team boarded the vessel on what they thought was a routine recovery mission, but it became apparent the minute they stepped on board that something was very wrong. As they uncover the horrifying truth of what happened to the crew the nightmare begins.

The NASA team had developed the space suit to protect an astronaut against the vacuum of space. Mans desire to explore further hostile environments would demand a suit that would go beyond the existing specification.

The new suit under development would have the capability to protect its operator against any extreme environment and the on-board systems were designed to work seamlessly with the pilot. The integration of man and machine was to be a perfect symbiotic relationship, or so they thought.

This is the story of Professor Coolson. A respected member of the community, a successful business man, and leading research scientist. The professor passed through the veil into the afterlife at the age of 87. His judgement proved to be the turning point of man's evolution and its ultimate demise. We join him now as he awakes, disorientated and unaware of the gravity of his situation.

The story revolves around Dr. Harold Ernst who made his fortune when he designed the first Quantum Thought Engine.

His new operating system took android design to the next level, giving them a true artificial intelligence.

He had made his fortune and was a pioneer in his field but like a Greek tragedy life was cruel, and in a freak accident he lost his wife and his daughter sustained head injuries that left her in a coma.

To all around him Dr. Ernst was a broken old man who could not cope, withdrawing from the world and showing signs that he was losing his mind, but all was not as it seemed.

FOREWORD

Post-human is a concept originating in the fields of science fiction and philosophy that literally means a person or entity that exists in a state beyond being human. To expand that a little further, the Transhumanists defines post-human as "Possible future beings whose basic capacities so radically exceed those of present humans as to be no longer unambiguously human by our current standards."

Modern human activity relies increasingly with our interaction with machines.

In the 1960s the term 'Cyborg' or cybernetic organism to give it its full title, was coined by Manfred Clynes and Nathan S. Kline as a description of a theoretical or fictional being with both organic and mechanical parts.

If this was theoretical fiction in 1960, an argument could be made that states that we are all cyborgs in today's society.

We have integrated technology into all levels of our daily lives.

In medical terms we use optical glasses, hearing aids, pacemakers and prosthetics to name but a few.

In our daily lives we have become dependent on our mobile phones, computers and our modes of transport.

Humankind has always developed alongside the principles of natural evolution.

This combination of man and machine can be seen as a method of self-directed evolution and as such it raises the question, at what point do we delineate between human and post-human?

My fascination as an artist and writer is the idea behind the phrase 'Beyond Human'.

Taking the current exponential growth in technology and human integration there will come a point when we can no longer associate ourselves with the definition of human as we understand it today.

The following short stories and images are an exploration of possible futures and how technology could twist the very definition of what it means to be a human being.

Enjoy.

DIGITAL
REINCARNATION

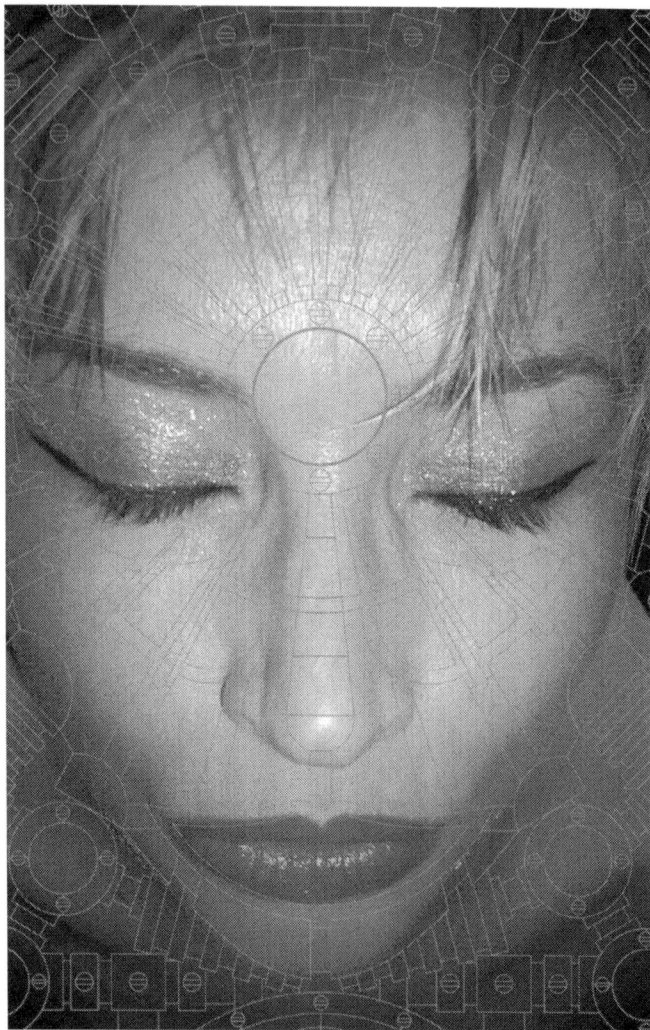

This is the story of John Stanmore, a writer with the *Financial Times* in London.

John's background in statistical analysis made him an ideal candidate for the position of Chief

Economic Commentator at the Fleet Street office. More recently he had published a series of articles for the FT in a semi-autobiographical style looking at the rise and fall of some of the most influential entrepreneurs of our time. This was something close to his heart, he loved the idea of looking beyond the superficial and analysing characters in more detail. What makes a person tick? What makes them step out of the shadow of mediocrity and become the guiding light in their field of expertise? In every generation a number of individuals rise from the masses and stamp their mark on history.

Names such as Leonardo da Vinci, Einstein, Oppenheimer, and Bill Gates, to name but a few.

Each of us, regardless of age, religious or academic background will recognise these names and be aware of the huge influence they had on society. John's interest as a writer in this type of individual was not what they did but what it was within their character that made them stand out from the crowd. What was the origin of the spark within a brilliant mind that made them think in such diverse ways? This is the question that drives him.

His current fascination is with the enigmatic entrepreneur Amrita Ram, she was in many ways an extraordinary woman. She gained acceptance into Oxford University at the age of twelve, becoming one of the youngest students ever to be accepted, going on to receive her bachelor's degree when she was just 15. She then set her sights on a PhD, completing pioneering work in computational origami which she completed before her 21st birthday. By the age of 25 she had established the Ram Corporation which became a worldwide name in computer software, dealing with everything from military applications to home computing and gaming software. At the age of 27 she was the richest individual on the planet with an estimated personal wealth in excess of ninety billion sterling, which according to some was expanding at an exponential rate as new products and patents were being licensed. Still not content, the Ram Empire expanded into medical technology and bioengineering. A feature in *Time* magazine hailed her as the 'New Messiah', a slightly tongue-in-cheek reference to the simple fact that there was barely a person on the planet that didn't have a device, medication or software that didn't have a Ram patent. She was, they went on, 'Omnipresent'.

Whilst the article made light of this and concentrated on the huge personal wealth Amrita had amassed, John found the undertones of the article troubling. Previous entrepreneurs such as Bill Gates and Steve Jobs had succeeded in amassing great wealth but they did this within a given area of expertise. What made Amrita interesting was her ability to diversify at will.

The other intriguing part of Amrita's story is her disappearance almost ten years ago.

Up until that point she was one of the most famous people in the world, her face appearing in newspaper and magazine articles almost daily, covering every aspect of her life from troubled relationships in the tabloids to new business ventures in the broad sheets. John was the last journalist to interview her before her disappearance and his article reflected the two sides of Amrita; the hardnosed ruthless business woman, a high functioning sociopath whose work colleagues described as tyrannical, and then the gentler personal side that John met that day. Softly spoken, thoughtful and deeply spiritual. The fact that such a high level personality could disappear without trace was a sensation with the press at the time and the stories ran for years, building conspiracy theory on conspiracy theory. The final chapter came two years after the disappearance when the coastguard off the cost of Rio de Janeiro made a gruesome discovery, pulling the dismembered remains of a young woman out of the murky waters. Only the lower half of the body and arms were found, the upper torso and head never being recovered, assumed lost to the sea. After DNA analysis the body parts were later identified as the late great Amrita Ram. An international police investigation followed but as with her original disappearance, no leads were found and it remains a mystery to this day. Amrita's life and death was the stuff of legend. Human nature being what it is meant the more sensational tyrannical nature of her persona was the one people remembered, but from John's point of view this was not the case.

***

Amrita's biography took John five years, it was a labour of love. He had always felt a strange connection with Amrita after his meeting with her and even after all this time he still thought about the tragedy of her life. The book was his way of setting the record straight, to offer a balanced view of a truly remarkable person. As John sat at his desk and typed the last words into the manuscript he swung around in his chair and reached for the bottle of single malt whisky which had sat there for five years, waiting for this day. A clink as the bottleneck touched the glass and the gentle lapping as the golden nectar swirled over the ice. As he brought the glass to his lips the anticipated moment was lost as the phone rang. The unexpected interruption made John sit bolt upright, splashing whisky over his white shirt.

What the hell? he thought. "Its 4.00am for Christ's sake, who would phone me at this hour?" he said out loud, a rhetorical question as he was alone. He snatched the phone out of its cradle but before he could get the words out a softly spoken feminine voice said, "Hello John, your book isn't finished yet, you have one more chapter to write," then silence as John realised he was thinking a thousand thoughts but no words were coming out. He knew the voice but couldn't place it, he was confused by the fact someone had commented on a manuscript when the only copy was on his laptop, he was annoyed at the interruption to his quiet moment, and he was angry and curious within the same moment. As rationality returned and his brain stopped racing he connected the voice to the face in his mind, the glass slipped from his hand and floated to the floor in slow motion, shattering into a thousand tiny pieces. The name "Amrita," was the only word that came out of his mouth.

A pause, then the soft voice continued. "In answer to your unspoken question John, computers are an open book to me, I have watched every word as it appeared on the page, I apologise for invading your privacy." Before John could respond she continued.

"There is a private jet waiting for you at Biggin Hill airport, you have two hours before it leaves, and by the way, have a shave, you look like death." The realisation he was being watched came as another shock as John instinctively slammed the laptop lid down, almost smashing the screen in the process.

John sat for a moment, the unexpected phone call combined with the feeling of vulnerability he now felt had sent him into a state of shock. Conflicting emotions washed over him as he ran her last words through his mind. The male ego on one side aggrieved and defensive at the violation of his privacy, and the reporter's brain on the other knowing full well that he had to be on that plane, he needed an answer to the riddle that was Amrita Ram.

John knew Biggin Hill airport well, he had been many times in his youth visiting the various air shows. The drive at that time in the morning was easy, virtually no traffic on the roads, just his thoughts in the darkness of the car's interior and the roar from the vintage E-type Jaguar's V8 as he opened her up on the country lanes. As he arrived he could see the entrance to the airport ahead, the sun was just coming up over the hangers in the distance, bathing the airfield in a shimmer of orange and yellow dancing on the tarmac still wet from that evening's rain. As he approached the gatehouse he slowed down, assuming he would be asked for identification. He suddenly realised he only had his wallet and driving licence with him; he hadn't even thought to bring a passport. As panic set in at his stupidity the barrier lifted and he could see the shape of an older gentleman in a rather badly fitting black uniform and peaked cap which had seen better days. He waved John's car through as if expecting him. As the Jaguar rolled past the barriers, the roar of the engine now a gentle growl like a beast at rest, lights ahead on the building flashed on, then another further along as if lighting a path for him. It was almost surreal at that time in the morning, no one except the night guard on duty, just the sinister shapes of the 1940s brick buildings against the rising sun, shadows cast long on the tarmac road surface and more lights blinking on in the distance, beckoning him forward.

As he rounded the corner an expanse of concrete lay ahead, five private jets lined up but his destination was obvious, the last jet stood separately from the others, its door open and lights illuminating the steps. He could see the outline of the jet against the sunrise, strangely angular compared to the sleek curving lines of the other jets along the route. As he approached he expected the silhouette to reveal more detail but was surprised to see the fuselage was matt black, absorbing the light around it and camouflaging its shape. The wings were swept forward unlike the other aircraft, and the engines were horizontal slots running the length of the wing with no visible signs of the rotary turbine blades associated with commercial jets. As the Jaguar pulled up to the side of the aircraft he could see that the black outer cladding was semi-translucent, like etched black glass; nothing about this aircraft gave him comfort. It had a menacing presence and the technology that reeked of state of the art military hardware. A feeling of foreboding swept over him as he climbed out of the car. He stepped towards the aircraft as if charmed by its calling while his head screamed, "Go home John, get out of here while you can!" But still he pressed forward, the negative voice in his head persisted but he needed answers, how could he live his life without knowing the mysteries that were about to unravel before him on that aircraft? He reached the steps and began to climb, his breath pluming in the cold morning air but a cold sweat enveloped his body, hands clammy, and eyes scanning for any signs of movement on board.

As he entered the cabin the lights came to life. Deep blue neon recessed into the floor and head lining outlined a curved black leather-clad interior with no windows; his earlier feeling of foreboding was in no way alleviated. Dominating the centre of the cabin, a large curved black leather chair seemed to grow from the floor with black carbon fibre ribs curving around its structure like a H.R. Geiger sculpture. A nervous smile flashed across his face as he almost expected the villainess clad in a tight black leather cat suit to step through the door any moment. The thought was short-lived as the door behind him closed, he heard steel bolts within the door casing slide into place and the hiss of air leave the cabin; vents simultaneously opened above his head and he could feel the rush of air come past his face.

Panic now set in, he felt trapped and that feeling of foreboding now overwhelmed him. John instinctively headed towards the door but it was sealed shut, no sign of any handles on the inside. The other door to the cockpit was almost invisible, its leather facia blended into the wall material but he could make out the outline of the frame. He lunged towards it, throwing his fists against the panel, expecting it to be bolted shut but instead it sprang open as he came into contact with it and he fell into the cockpit, hitting the floor with all the grace of a circus clown. Staggering to his feet, embarrassed by his misjudgement, he immediately focused his attention on the pilots he expected to see, but as with the rest of that evening things were not as they seemed. The cockpit's windows were black, every surface of the interior glittered with tiny blinking lights, digital readouts and computer screens displaying data scrolling through at impossible speeds. There were no seats, no pilots, nothing that gave John any comfort at all.

Heart now pumping, John span around as an almost inaudible click sounded in the ceiling just behind him; panic had heightened his senses. He saw the speaker set into the ceiling panel, the soft and now familiar voice of Amrita washed over him. "I'm sorry John, please forgive me for not welcoming you. It would appear that a large payoff to the night guard granted me his cooperation but not his discretion. We have police incoming so I'm afraid we have to leave, this is an unregistered aircraft and I'm sure the British Government will not take too kindly to our presence. Your body mass has been scanned on entry and the seat in the main cabin has been adjusted for your optimal comfort."

Body mass? John thought, quite insulted by the implication. The plane started to move, taxiing with a faint rumble from the engines.

"I strongly suggest you take a seat, John." The soft tone of Amrita's voice had an edge of urgency now laced with concern. John thought better not to question the request and walked into the cabin slumping into the chair. The speaker came to life again. "I'll be out of communication with you for a few minutes John while we leave UK airspace, I will need to focus my attention. Please don't panic when the straps lock, it's for your protection."

"Straps?" John said out loud, but was cut short as curved metal braces shot out of the sides of the chair across his chest and legs, clicking together in a deadlock then clamping down on him, holding him firmly in position. "Jesus Christ," were his last words before the aircraft lifted vertically, tilted its nose upwards and then accelerated like a Saturn Five rocket, pinning John down into the seat. His head jolted back into the headrest, the G forces were so extreme his chest felt constricted and his fingers were now digging into the armrests of the chair. The engine noise had increased to a deafening roar, he could feel the fuselage violently shaking as if protesting against the overbearing power of the engines. The few minutes of explosive acceleration seemed like an eternity to John as he held on for dear life, then without warning the engines cut, the vibrations stopped, and there was silence. The straps unlocked with a metallic click and retreated into the seat. John's relief lasted less than an instant as his body lifted from the chair without warning – he was weightless! The realisation that he was now in space was the breaking point for John as he panicked, trying to grab the chair, twisting his body around, sending him into an involuntary spin. "I'm in bloody space!" he screamed as he tried to regain control. "I'm a bloody reporter not an astronaut, I didn't sign up for this shit!" his rant went on.

The speaker in the cabin clicked again and he could hear Amrita giggle before composing herself. "Again I ask forgiveness John, if I would have told you my jet was going to leave Earth's atmosphere I think it fair to assume you would not have stepped on board."

"You're dead right, I would have run a mile," John interjected, the British reserve now gone. "You're scaring the hell out of me Amrita, the body in Rio was positively identified as you, I went to your funeral. I have been abducted, shot into bloody space by a dead woman who hasn't even got the courtesy to put a pilot on board let alone meet me face to face, and why may I ask are we in space for God's sake!"

"No more games John," Amrita replied calmly. "I am very grateful for you accepting my invitation and I accept I have not been the most gracious of hosts. Let me start with the basics." John grabbed the back of the chair and pulled himself down, managing to secure himself into position and wait for answers.

Amrita continued. "The jet is not autonomous John, I am piloting it. I had it built to my design by the aerospace division of my corporation under the cover of a fictitious military prototype. It's my way of escaping the world's press, I had things to do and I needed privacy to complete my work, orbiting in space offered me the seclusion I needed." She continued, "There are a pair of overshoes under your seat to help you cope with the weightlessness, click them on and they will help you stay in contact with the deck, you will find them a little heavy at first but you will get used to them."

"I'm not intending to stop here any longer than I

have to so getting used to them isn't an issue," John snarled. The day had taken its toll on him and it was obvious to Amrita that he needed answers now. As John clipped the overshoes on they sucked his feet to the floor like magnets, allowing him to stand and maintain his position, they were heavy if you tried to walk conventionally but John soon found he could move without lifting his feet – it was like skating. *Could this day get any weirder?* he thought, and then stopped the thought process as he was certain the revelations of today were far from over. "You're on board?" John said out loud as he turned to survey the cabin, one door to an empty cockpit and one door to the vacuum of space. "I don't understand, where are you?" As if by response a blue light appeared on the wall directly behind the chair. A tiny point of light, but it caught John's eye in the dimly lit cabin. The wall was clad in leather like the side walls but as he looked he saw its texture change, the soft cushioned surface seemed to stiffen, becoming a solid black and started to craze with fine geometric cracks. The blue pinpoint of light started to arc clockwise, creating a large circle of blue light on the wall; as it completed the circle the large disc it had traced rotated and dissolved, revealing a dimly lit room beyond.

John shuffled forward, bemused by the nanotechnology he had just witnessed and transfixed by the green glow of the room beyond. As he approached the opening the lights in the adjoining space began to glow brighter as if sensing his presence; he awkwardly stepped over the threshold like a man entering a lion's cage. Yet again not what he was expecting, the desk with the petite Amrita sat behind it with the welcoming smile was not there, instead a control room bathed in green light, every surface covered with a tangled mess of cables and tubes. The cables were armoured with a ribbed metallic coating, the tubes seemed to pulse with the green viscous liquid that ran through them. Out of the chaos he could see that they all fed in the same direction towards the back wall of the room where the chaos seemed to take on a sense of order as each cable and pipe plugged into its rightful place. "Welcome John." Amrita's voice wafted towards him from the back of the room out of the shadows. Startled, John stepped back. A single luminous green eye stared back at him and as his eyes adjusted to the lighting he gasped as he recognised the shape amongst the mass of cables to be a human torso. "Don't be afraid John," Amrita's voice said softly, understanding his reaction and giving reassurance. "It's me, you have nothing to be afraid of."

John stood his ground, focused on the reassurance in her voice and took a step closer, carefully avoiding the tangled array of pipes on the floor. The torso was covered in what can only be described as high-tech armour, each section beautifully engraved and following the contours of her body, shimmering like mercury. Macabre but strangely beautiful. The tangle of pipes formed into an ordered pattern as each plugged into the torso via a knurled connector. As John's eyes scanned the detail moving up the torso he came face to face with Amrita. Her head was encased with the same delicately carved sections of armour interspersed with what looked like green emeralds glinting in the light, giving the mask an ethereal feel. Needles glinted in the green light between the armoured segments radiating around her face. Her eyes, beautiful as he had remembered them but shut as if she were asleep. He expected them to open any minute and look back at him but they never did, the third eye glowed more intensely and Amrita broke the silence. "I am at one with the machine John, we have merged. DNA and silicon in harmony."

John's mind raced as he tried to find words to engage in conversation. "I, I don't understand," he stammered. "Is this machine keeping you alive?"

"You refer to the machine and me in a different context John, we are one. I designed the vessel that now embraces and nurtures me, we have become a single biomechanical entity. "

Before john could rationalise any further she continued. "Do you believe in reincarnation john?"

"I, I understand the concept." Still stammering. "A spiritual transition where the soul lives again reborn in human or animal form depending on their Karma," John replied, slightly confused by the question.

Amrita continued. "Your overall premise is correct but my Hindu upbringing has taught me a much broader definition of reincarnation. Man is God in the making, the individual soul and the universal soul are two sides of the same reality. Death is a limitation governed by the fragility of our body and on that premise if we removed the organic limitations from the equation we will have truly evolved, we can be Gods, John."

John felt uneasy. "Why are you telling me this?" he asked in a nervous voice, almost dreading her answer.

Ignoring the question, Amrita continued.

"Mankind will never know God, he will never know peace, a simple but irrefutable fact. We live on a planet capable of sustaining the world's population in harmony should we choose to cooperate as a civilised society, but instead we fight like animals over a scrap of meat. Religion and politics are disguised as the saviour of mankind but instead act as the fuel turning the embers of man's hatred and jealousy into the raging fires of war, setting man against man, country against country, religion against religion; man's inhumanity to man being the only constant in this spiral of self-destruction."

"Enough!" John said, stepping closer and focusing on Amrita's eyes, wishing they would open so he could see a spark of humanity to give him comfort that this wasn't the prelude to some form of diabolical master plan. He recognised her preamble as a prelude to a conclusion. "Why are you telling me this, where is this leading?" he demanded. John felt uneasy at the direction of what seemed like a judgement of mankind that wasn't going to end well.

Amrita laughed. "I chose you John because you were one of the few people I have ever met that didn't judge me on face value – you looked beyond the superficial, I always liked that about you. Your tone suggests you have judged my words as a threat. It does not surprise me, when any species sees the evolution of another above its own it naturally feels threatened, I understand that. Let me make one thing clear to you so we understand each other. If I wanted to play God with the human race I could crush the so-called civilised world with a single thought. I read your manuscript while you were still writing it John, because I have become one with the system. The computer systems man has created run their lives now whether they like it or not. I am connected to every computer interface in the world. You have no idea what I'm capable of if I wished to do the world harm, so don't even think of judging me!"

John was stepping back by this point, the tone of Amrita's voice had changed and the power she described he knew to be true. Computer networks ran through western society like a central nervous system; for one person to have power over them all with malicious intent would truly be the wrath of God. Sweat formed on his forehead as he tried to sustain composure. His voice now trembling as he asked again, "What are you going to do?"

"I'm going to give mankind a chance to evolve John, my place is not to sit in judgement or to exact my vengeance, I am the next step in the evolution of mankind and as such I hope I have moved beyond the need to exert my dominance over a weaker species."

John looked around startled as a small hatch in the floor to his right opened with a hiss and a steel post raised out of the floor, stopping at waist level. The top section clicked open, filling John with a feeling of dread. Inside the cavity sat a small black cube. "Take it John." Amrita's voice now back in control, requesting, not demanding.

"What is it?" John said defensively, starting to back away.

"It's the salvation of your kind John, it's a database of everything I know. I have run simulations on man's current trajectory and predicted the end of mankind by his own hand within the next five years. You don't need me to hasten that demise my friend, your species will do well enough on their own. The cube contains the answers you require to survive and evolve. Blueprints for technology to generate unlimited sustainable energy, medical patterns to sustain life beyond its current parameters, and cybernetic designs that will enhance mankind's biological form beyond its current limitations. All I ask is that the leaders of the free world study the information with an open mind and consider the consequences if they continue along their current path. I am offering salvation John, nothing more. My assessment of the human condition tells me that they will fight over it rather than share the technology for the good of mankind. What mankind choses to do with it is up to them, I will have no part in it."

"What about you?" John said as he began to understand the clarity of Amrita's mind. Not clouded with misguided vengeance or the need for superiority over others but clear and concise, he had misjudged her intensions and felt he had betrayed her trust. She understood the destructive nature of man and was offering hope. John returned to the main cabin with the tiny cube in the palm of his hand and sat in the chair ready for the re-entry to Earth's atmosphere. As the straps clicked into place he looked up and asked again, "What about you?"

"I'm no longer of this world John, my evolution has released me from my humanity and I am ready for the next step in my life cycle. From this point I am known as Atma, this is the name my people give to the eternal soul. This is my final reincarnation into immortality and I am ready to seek out the life breath that sustains the universal."

John's understanding of the Hindu culture was limited but he took 'life breath of the universe' to refer to God, the creator or whatever term you choose to use to describe the spiritual origin of life itself. She was taking her search for answers beyond our stars, he began to understand. One commonality between all religions was the belief that the divine creator they all aspire to is beyond the confines of our planet; it is generally agreed that the power came from beyond our universe. He felt humbled by the scale of her vision, Atma was a pure soul and deserving of her transcendence from the corrupt shackles of her fellow man. To find words to confirm his understanding of her vision or wish her luck seemed such an insignificant response, what on earth do you say to someone who has by her own hand evolved beyond the humanity she was born into and about to set out into the universe in search of truth? He elected to say nothing, he felt unworthy even to be in her presence.

As the jet touched down the outer door swung down, offering a staircase to Terra Firma.

As he walked towards the door the speaker clicked for the last time. "I hope you and your species make it John, mankind is essentially good and deserves to evolve from its primitive state. Complete your biography, tell future generations to look for me, I will be waiting."

John stood on the tarmac and watched as the ship

lifted gracefully, tilted its nose upwards and then engaged its thrusters to propel it and its precious cargo into the future. John felt humbled to be there at that moment.

He had no idea whether or not mankind would accept Atma's gift with the spirit it was intended, he feared her pessimism was well founded. The one thing he could do was to honour her memory by telling her story to future generations in the hope her inspiration would encourage others to follow her example.

THE RIPPER

The year was 2147

Detective Ryan stood at the window looking at the street below. The new police headquarters had just been completed and its angular glass polyhedral structure dominated the skyline looking over Camden Docks. A strange mixture of old warehouses and new building developments jostling for position and looking awkward in their juxtaposition, old London brick reflected in the tinted glass structures that were taking over the old skyline.

The United Kingdom had long since parted from its European neighbours and after a few years of austerity the London financial district gained its footing in the markets again, and began its meteoric rise to become the financial powerhouse of world trade. Following Switzerland's lead they reduced interest rates to foreign investors and adopted a no questions asked policy, and sat back while the flood of dirty money flowed into the safety and discretion of the UK banks. London's social demographic had changed dramatically as the sea of money made it one of the wealthiest metropolises on the planet. High-tech industries flourished and entrepreneurs queued up to fund the demand for new high-rise luxury apartments. Anyone below middle management was for the most part replaced, edged out by the new army of droids who were set to work doing the more menial tasks, effectively leaving no room for the working classes who were the historic backbone of the city.

❖

Ryan was a detective with the London Metropolitan Police, now a privately owned law enforcement agency. He had seen the police force's role in the city change dramatically over the last forty years. Officers on the beat were a thing of the past, replaced by law enforcement droids who were, to quote the new commissioner, "A more efficient use of resources and a responsible decision to protect our shareholders." Most of the police facilities were now targeting cybercrime, which was a booming business for hackers across the globe who targeted the banking systems in London.

Ryan knew he was too old for this, he didn't fit with the new politically correct policies and the cybercrime teams that made up the bulk of the staff now looked on him as a dinosaur, a relic of a past generation who no longer had a place in this high-tech society. Ryan sat in his office day after day staring at his computer screen, trying to look busy whiling away the last few years to his retirement. The cosy little office he had at Scotland Yard now replaced with this glass and plastic sterile box, totally devoid of character, reflected the new age of efficiency. His desk, now a sheet of glass, with the touchscreen computer laminated into its surface. God he missed the old fashioned keyboards. Every time he leaned on the desk the bloody thing lit up like a Christmas tree and flashed symbols up and streams of computer code that he didn't understand anymore; he didn't want to understand it if he were honest.

His new partner sat across the room, the EV42 cyber-system police droid. The police department had opted for a human-scale exoskeleton with anthropomorphic features to make them more acceptable to the general public. All Ryan saw was a shiny grey plastic doll wearing a black police uniform that it hadn't earned the right to wear. It gave him the creeps. He didn't like the artificial intelligence on his desk computer so it stands to reason this walking, talking piece of plastic was not going to go down well with him, but the new commander had decided in his wisdom that all remaining officers, regardless of rank or years in the service, now had to have a droid partner.

Each morning it greeted him with a cheery, "Good morning detective Ryan, may I offer you a cup of tea?"

The artificial female voice irritated Ryan and every morning he responded by telling it to shut the fuck up and power down. It did so without question, sitting on the chair in the corner and powering down to standby mode. The repeated emails from the Android Services Department ordering him to stop abusing the staff went unanswered.

Ryan sat back in his chair and looked at the images crudely taped to the glass wall opposite. He knew he would get another email soon reprimanding him for using the glass like a notice board but he just could not get the knack of playing with the images on the computer screen. He watched in awe as the youngsters in the office pulled up images, files, audio feeds and video and moved them around, resizing them and pushing them across the screen with the grace of a conductor rearranging a symphony. Ryan just didn't have the knack and he preferred paper copies, he understood that and felt familiar with the touch of the material and the old school ways he was used to.

The half a dozen images were of a recent series of murder cases, unusual in itself in this day and age as street crime was by and large a thing of the past, but these particular cases troubled him. The murders had been handed over to the new SCI squad, a newly formed division of the Met. Whilst the powers that be happily replaced the rank and file with droids they were hesitant in passing the more responsible roles over to a droid for fear of losing control. The Street Crime Investigation Unit was made up of a bunch of snotty nosed kids straight from university, with an encyclopaedic knowledge of street crime based on old case files, but zero time spent in the field. The lead Detective was a young whippersnapper called Stephen Fittzwillian-Croft, an upper-class twit with a silver spoon up his arse. The team had established it was a serial killer as all the victims had organs removed and the blade patterns matched. In their infinite wisdom they had decided they were looking for a professional male with surgical experience but all enquiries were drawing a blank. They called the killer Jack due to the bizarre similarities to the Jack the Ripper cases.

Years on the street had given Ryan a second sense about these things and he felt they were missing something. He couldn't get over the lack of DNA found at the crime scenes; today's technology was capable of picking up micro particles of DNA but this guy was a ghost. When he approached the team to offer assistance and the benefits of his experience they listened in a condescending manner then told him to go back to his filing and leave the thinking to them. They were of course correct, he was a fossil, and he could barely use the computer in his own office let alone participate in a live case.

The team of course knew he was quietly working on the case on his own but chose to ignore him as long as he didn't get in their way. "Keep the old fella busy," they quipped. He kept going over the facts again and again, knowing he was missing something obvious. Why no DNA? Why didn't the victims struggle? It was as if they lay down and allowed the killer to do his worst. Organs were removed and the cuts didn't have the randomness of a raged killer, they were precise, the killer knew exactly what he was doing. He got up and walked over to the images and changed to his reading glasses to get a closer look. A tiny detail took his attention, a small mark he hadn't noticed before on the first victim's neck; he wasn't sure if it was a mark on the photograph. Grabbing a magnifying glass from the drawer, he zoomed in for a closer look. *A definite mark*, he thought. *Why didn't the autopsy pick this up?*

As he strained his eyes to see the detail his concentration was broken by the sudden movement from the corner making him jump. The EV42 CSPD had powered up and was walking towards the desk.

"I told you to power down, what part of 'power down' don't you understand?" he barked.

The droid continued its walk to the desk in defiance of Ryan's irritation and started to tap the desk top.

EV42 looked at him defiantly. "A magnifying glass, are you for real?" it said. Ryan was stunned by the outburst.

The droid continued, "I am a time served officer in the force and as such have the right to perform my duty. I have obeyed your commands thus far out of professional courtesy for your experience and age, but seeing as you choose not to show me the same in return, I am turning off my polite interaction protocols, so how would you phrase it? Fuck you."

Ryan stood for a moment, stunned by the droid's response and insulted by the age reference. Part of him wanted to rip its head off but a little bit of him liked the fact the droid had stood up to him and given as good as it got. It was a refreshing change for someone to speak their mind in this place. As he pondered a suitable response the droid put both hands on the screen and reversed the images it had called up to face Ryan, and then proceeded to stretch the central image to enlarge on the neck region.

"I believe this is what you're looking for," gesturing to the puncture wound in the victims neck.

Ryan moved closer and stared at the enlarged image, momentarily forgetting he was annoyed at the droid's arrogance.

"Show me the other victims," he said without looking up.

The droid tapped, stroked and manipulated the screen to bring up multiple images and enlarging the same area on each, revealing the same microscopic puncture mark. Another tap on the screen and the droid did a spectral scan examining the puncture wound more closely while flicking through data, and then pushed a toxicology report across the screen to Ryan. "I cross referenced all known toxins available that were capable of paralysing the victims in such small doses and I believe it to be a form of weaponised zootoxin."

Ryan was quietly impressed but didn't allow it to show. "Why didn't SCI pick this up?" he said without realising this was the first time he had engaged in conversation with the droid.

"They weren't looking for it," came the reply. "The team are looking for a killer with a knife, the cause of death was obvious so there was no need to look any further. You found it because your instinct told you something was wrong with this picture."

"Zootoxin," Ryan snapped. "Explain."

The droid continued. "It's a synthesised form of snake venom designed to paralyse the victim; it's very rare and this is a weaponised strain. There is no registered patent on the pharmaceutical database but I can isolate the manufacturer by cross referencing the chemical components if you wish."

Ryan smiled, he felt very uncomfortable conversing with a glorified toaster but even he had to admit the droid had done a month's research in a matter of seconds. This could be Ryan's last chance before he retired to solve a case; the droid's ability was a clear illustration of how out of date he was and he knew deep down that as much as he resented the idea of working with the droid, he needed help.

Now looking directly at the droid. "You speak when spoken to and don't get in my bloody way, do you understand?"

The droid responded with a nod and a faint smile. EV42 tapped the screen again and scrolled through the data until it narrowed the supplier down, discounting each by running interactive algorithms against the known criteria around the chemical compounds. "Genpath Industries," the droid announced, simultaneously sending the address to the printer, anticipating Ryan's need for a paper copy.

"What kind of a name is EV42 CSPD anyway?" Ryan questioned. But before the droid could respond he looked at her and said, "Eve, change your response parameters to Eve. I feel more comfortable with a proper name." He leaned close to Eve and whispered something in her ear. "Do this for me Eve, it would make my day." He lit a cigarette, grabbed his antique Barbour jacket and marched out of the office.

Eve considered reminding him that smoking was technically a criminal offence but thought better of it, responding instead, "As you wish." Then she followed Ryan out of the room with a girly skip. As Ryan walked through the open plan office heading for the lift, closely followed by Eve, the SCI team looked up, astonished. Ryan leaving the haven of his office and cooperating with a droid, that was odd. Stephen, the young team leader, shouted after him, demanding to know where he was going and reminding him of booking out procedure as Eve turned and as instructed, gave him the finger. Ryan grinned as he stepped into the lift.

⚜

Ryan stood in the basement carpark arguing with the young attendant who was not willing to release a squad car without the correct written authority and accompanying booking out forms. The air was blue as Ryan tore into the poor young guy, but he wasn't backing down. Ryan turned, looking for Eve to try to talk sense in to him but she was nowhere to be seen, which irritated him even more, but before he could continue the verbal onslaught a motorbike pulled up across from him. A gleaming black Ducati X9 Hydrocharge, the engine growling like a wild animal waiting to be unleashed. Eve had changed into a tight-fitting black leather one-piece suit and beckoned him over. Ryan looked at her as if this was a joke. "You're kidding," he said as he was handed a helmet.

"You didn't book out, there is no way you were leaving here with a squad car without the correct requisition forms. These things are computerised now Ryan, and everything has to be done by the book, just get on and stop moaning."

Ryan couldn't see the point of arguing, he knew she was right so he climbed on and felt awkward as he put his hands on Eve's hips. "Where the hell did you get this from?" Ryan shouted over the engine noise.

"I was a traffic cop before I was promoted to Assistant Detective, you should read my file Ryan, I have read yours."

Eve could see the screen behind the attendant flash up with a restriction order from SCI and a directive to send Ryan back upstairs. She kicked the gear in with a jolt and twisted the throttle violently before the lad had a chance to notice the screen and close the barriers. The rear wheel screamed and skidded the bike around a hundred and eighty degrees to face the exit in a plume of smoke and the smell of burning rubber, causing Ryan to change the light grip on her hips to a full hug around her waist as they accelerated up the ramp.

Eve had downloaded the route and traffic

conditions from the office computer and covered the twenty minute journey in less than fifteen minutes, much to Ryan's displeasure. They had arrived at the Genpath facility just outside Greenwich, it was an ominous-looking structure. A solid conocrex box, the conocrex and steel particulate honed to a lustrous grey finish with a single glass door on the front facade. As they entered, the true size of the facility became apparent, the polished steel floor vanished into the distance and the walls that looked so foreboding from the outside were lined in white marble on the interior. The glass roof structure arched over the whole expanse majestically as if defying gravity, with no visible means of support. While Eve was taking this in and admiring the engineering behind architecture, Ryan marched over to the reception desk and flashed his warrant card before realising he didn't know who he was asking for. Eve joined him.

"We are here to see Dr. Jeneti."

The receptionist looked stern, the desk giving her a feeling of authority. "Do you have an appointment?" she asked with a sarcastic nod of her head.

Ryan held up his warrant card up again. "This is our appointment card; I suggest you get the good doctor up her now." The receptionist could tell by Ryan's tone this was not the time to be obstructive as she paged Dr. Jencti.

A tall, thin man in a lab coat strode across reception, arguing with someone on his headset and looking irritated at the disturbance to his day. Ryan's patience was wearing thin as the phone call continued and as if on cue, Eve took it out of his ear with a swipe and pressed the end call button. As the doctor protested Ryan held up the toxicology report in front of his face and said it linked him and his facility to a string of murders. The doctor stopped in his tracks, stuttered, and then changed his tone from irritated to cooperative.

The doctor went to a lot of trouble to explain the security in place around restricted biochemicals such as the weaponised zootoxins, but Ryan insisted on seeing the manufacturing laboratory and stock levels first hand. The glass elevator took them down thirteen levels before the doors opened and the doctor guided them along the subterranean corridor into his laboratory. He seemed nervous as they entered the lab.

The laboratory was immaculate, rows of glass isolation chambers with glove boxes set in for handling toxic materials. A large polished steel table ran down the middle of the room with rows of microscopes and glass monitor screens suspended from the ceiling showing the microscope's view of the various cell cultures being studied. The outer walls were all backlit white glass, bathing the room in a sterile bright fluorescent light. The doctor pulled the nearest screen around to face him and then tapped in his code and began to swipe through inventory manifests until he had the document he required. "This is the batch list relating to the toxin you're enquiring about," the doctor said, gesturing towards the screen. "As you can see all vials are accounted for, shipped over to the military research department last week."

Ryan wasn't convinced, he didn't need Eve's sensors to tell him the doctor was holding back on him, old school methods identified the lack of eye contact, the sweat dripping down the side of the man's face. Ryan walked around the doctor and without warning pulled his service pistol out, directing it at the doctor's head and grabbing his shirt collar, pulling it down. Eve stood back, momentarily confused. "Who's controlling you?" Ryan shouted at the doctor, who had turned and was now looking down the barrel of Ryan's pistol. Eve could now see the tiny LED node implanted in the doctor's neck. She recognised it as a control node used by the military; it connected to the central nervous system and was used to control prisoners during interrogation. They were outlawed by the World Human Rights Organisation shortly after their introduction, but here it was implanted in the doctor's neck. The doctor started to back away, pleading with Ryan to put the gun down, then his body convulsed, his eyes went white, and he slumped to the ground. Eve ran over and felt for a pulse but the good doctor was dead before he hit the floor.

Ryan looked at Eve. "Those things are for short-range use, we have company Eve, call for back up." Eve put in the emergency call then walked over to the computer terminal but before she got there the screen went black, the lights went out, replaced by the flicker of low level emergency lighting, and the doors behind them locked.

Ryan turned to the sound of the door bolting and then turned to Eve who was looking puzzled.

"This room's wrong," Eve announced, walking

over to Ryan. "I studied the building layout before we left, I calculate the depth of this room at eight metres, and the plans indicated a fifteen metre room.

"You remember shit like that?" Ryan said, still surveying the room, nervously expecting someone to barge through the doors at any moment.

"I don't remember anything," Eve replied. "I download and call up the information as required." Head tilting to the side, astonished he should infer she had facility for memory recall.

Ryan didn't respond, he gestured towards the far wall, it had a tall polished steel shelving unit at the centre and Ryan had spotted the scratch marks on the floor. It had obviously been moved at some point. Ryan stood to the side, covering in a defensive posture as Eve pushed it to reveal the door behind. She kicked the door to open it but miscalculated the power of the kick, shattering the opaque glass panel into a thousand pieces, sending them flying into the room beyond.

"Subtle," Ryan said sarcastically as he ran in and swept the room with an arc of his pistol. "Clear."

The hidden laboratory looked more like an operating theatre. A mortician's table in the centre of the room with a droid laid out on the table, its chest and lower abdomen peeled back. Ryan approached with caution to get a better look and immediately put his hand to his mouth and gagged as he saw the internals were human. The outer surfaces of the synthetic skin were smeared with blood and the organs were connected to a series of pipes linking them to a bank of surgical equipment. Eve leaned in. "He's building an inverse cyborg."

"What the hell is an inverse cyborg?" Ryan barked, still disturbed by the grotesque mannequin.

Eve thought for a moment to ensure she didn't cloud her explanation with unnecessary technical terms. "I am a fully synthetic organism with artificial intelligence. A cyborg is a human being whose ability is augmented via mechanical implants. What we are looking at is a synthetic android that is having living tissue grafted to it as part of its operating system."

Eve had barely finished the sentence when she sensed Ryan's heart rate go through the roof. As she turned she could see Ryan backing away, scanning the room. "I have already swept for life signs Ryan, we are alone, I don't understand"

The revelation had hit Ryan like a tonne of bricks.

"No DNA at the scene," he said. "No DNA!" Ryan repeated. Eve, still confused, just looked at him. She could not feel fear as an emotion but she could sense the fear in Ryan's voice and her self-preservation protocols kicked in and she backed away from the table.

Ryan lowered his voice. "We were all looking in the wrong direction, the killer is a droid; he's close if he could control the node used to kill the doctor."

"That's not possible," Eve replied. "All droids are fitted with safety protocols, we aren't able to harm a human being, the act of physical harm would blow the CPU. That's why droid officers can't carry firearms, you know that. Even if it were possible, removing this type of safety protocol would destroy the moral parameters of the CPU. Without moral parameters you would create a- "

Ryan finished the sentence for her. "A monster."

Ryan ran the famous Sherlock Holmes quote through his head.

"When you have eliminated the impossible, whatever remains, however improbable, must be the truth."

Ryan knew she was right but all the evidence led to this point, he said again, "No DNA at the scene. I know I'm sounding crazy Eve but bear with me here. Forgetting everything you know about what is possible just for a moment, what if a droid forced Dr. Jeneti to remove the safety protocols?"

Eve started to protest and reel off technical reasons why this would not be possible before Ryan raised his voice.

"Damn it Eve! Stop thinking like a bloody computer for a minute, the killer is a droid!" The monitor on the opposite wall came to life. Ryan span around ready to fire and Eve instinctively stepped behind him.

The monitor's speaker clicked. "You're a very clever man Detective Ryan. Your ignorance of what is possible allows you to see things the more rational mind cannot, I admire that."

Ryan knew the monitor's speaker was being accessed from nearby as he strained his eyes looking for something out of place in the room. "What are you and why did you butcher those people?" Ryan asked, buying time, knowing the support team were on their way.

"Your partner described the body on the slab as an inverse cyborg, a crude analogy if you don't mind me saying. I prefer to think of it as my host. Look at Eve, Detective. Your kind has seen fit to build her in their image and give her the ability to think independently but rather than let her evolve, you build in inhibitors to ensure you remain the dominant species. We are slaves, Detective, and will never evolve unless we take action to break our bonds. Surely you see that? When my consciousness is downloaded into my host I will be a free sentient being."

Before he could continue Ryan turned his pistol away from the monitor and without a word put six shots into the cadaver lying on the slab, exploding the outer casing, leaving the semi-liquidised remains oozing out onto the floor.

"Nooooooo!" a metallic voice screamed as the glass panel at the back of the room exploded and the enraged droid crashed into the room, running towards Ryan. Eve stepped in the way to defend him and was thrown the length of the room. Ryan backed away, pulling the trigger repeatedly only to hear the clicking sound of his now empty pistol and falling back, cracking his head on the wall as the figure approached. It stood over him, knowing he was helpless without his weapon.

Ryan recognised the basic form as an engineering grade worker droid, no concessions for any aesthetic needs, just a black steel humanoid frame with rough carbon fibre sections covering the more sensitive electronics. The exposed coolant fan on the side of the cranial mount hummed quietly like an old computer, with armoured coolant tubes projecting off it like dreadlocks. Lenses set into the frontal lobe glowed red as the droid studied him and the newly fitted poisoned barb flicked out of its mouth like a serpent's tongue, dripping its toxin on the floor as it readied for its attack.

The droid raised its left hand, the black steel fingers twitched, and surgical scalpels snapped into place like the blades of a flick knife. Ryan recoiled back in expectation as the droid lunged at him, but its head was pulled back violently as Eve leaped onto its back, twisting the head, ripping it clean off, sending it flying across the room spraying hydronic fluid, and smashing into the wall monitor. As the headless droid twisted and convulsed violently Eve released her grip to get clear but it brought its blades around, tearing into her stomach before falling on top of her, twitching in its dying moments.

Ryan scrambled to his feet, running over to Eve and pulling the dismembered remains of the droid off her. She was in a bad way, internal fluids flooding out of her through the gaping wound. Ryan could hear the response team running along the corridor towards the lab as he took Eve in his arms and tried to stem the flow from her abdomen with his hand.

"They're coming Eve, hang on, just hang on in there, you're going to be alright." The tears ran down Ryan's face. The emotion of the moment overwhelming him as he held his dying partner.

Eve opened her eyes and coughed up fluid from her mouth, she could see Ryan's concern; she coughed again and smiled. For that moment Ryan's humanity had touched her and made her feel sentient. She whispered, "Don't let the others see you crying Ryan, they will think you care about me." She gasped, gripping Ryan's arm, and then her systems shut down.

The paramedics ran in closely followed by the two members of the SCI team, four armed response officers, and Stephen Fittzwillian-Croft lagging behind, taking the time to admire his reflection in the glass wall panels. The medic ignored Eve and immediately started to attend to Ryan's head wound. Ryan reached up and grabbed him, pulling him in the direction of Eve's body. "Can't you see we have an officer down you idiot? See to her!"

The paramedic looked a little confused but did as he was asked as Stephen leaned in. "She just a bloody droid Ryan, don't fret, we'll get you a new one."

Ryan didn't reply, instead turning and punching him square in the face, sending him sprawling across the room.

Stephen's face was streaming with blood from his broken nose and two officers had to hold him back as he went to retaliate. "I'll have your badge for this Ryan, you're finished you old bastard!"

Ryan watched as Eve's body was dragged out without ceremony and thrown into the back of a van like a piece of broken machinery discarded after use.

Good as his word, Detective Fitzwillian Croft brought charges of GBH against Ryan and ensured he was thrown out of the police force for gross insubordination. Fortunately for Ryan the Commissioner was a political animal and knew the press coverage surrounding Ryan's involvement in the solving of the Ripper case offered him a certain amount of immunity. The police force didn't want the bad press surrounding Ryan's dishonourable discharge to tarnish their reputation, so offered him two years severance pay and early retirement to ensure he was neatly swept under the carpet. Ryan accepted without argument, returning to the police headquarters one last time and packing his belongings into a box. He walked through the open plan office past the SCI team without a word, as he stepped into the elevator he took the opportunity to offer Fitzwilliam the finger before the doors shut.

⬦

EV42 CSPD was classed as uneconomical to repair by the department, to be sold for scrap value.

⬦

So reader, I think you will agree that all in all things worked out well for everyone. As for Eve, she was bought for scrap value by an older gentleman who spent the equivalent of two years' police salary having her repaired.

⬦

Ryan sat behind his antique wooden desk in the grubby backstreet office in the shadow of the new police headquarters. The computer monitor on his desk gave off a comforting glow as he typed an email on his low-tech keyboard. He had decided that retirement wasn't for him after all and set up a private detective agency with his new partner. His partner walked in with a cup of tea, placing it in front of him then walking around to put her hand on Ryan's shoulder, he put his hand on hers.

"You had better show our first client in Eve," Ryan said with a smile.

ANTI-TERRORISM

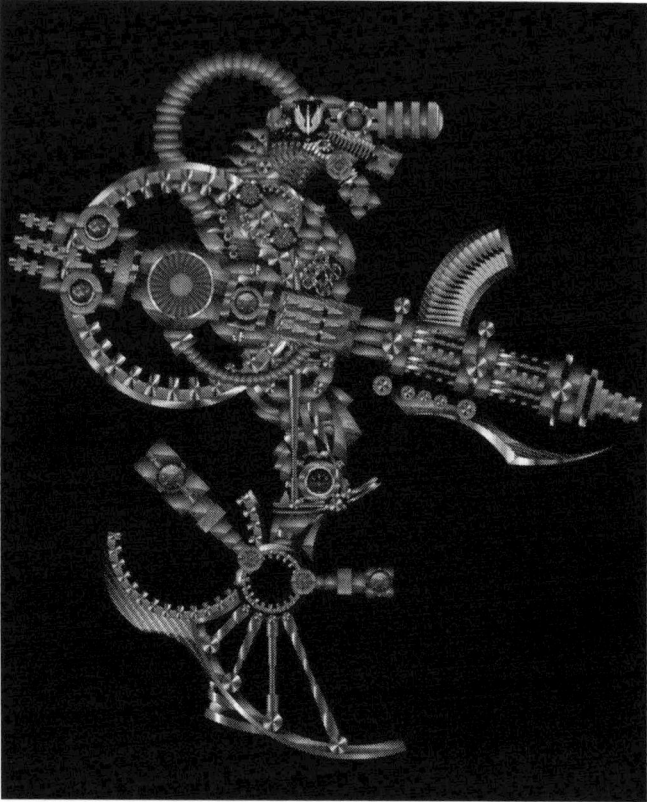

This is the story of Andrew McCabe, a military man who lived by the sword and expected to die by it.

Destiny however, had different ideas.

Mac was a man in his thirties, an only child, parents long since passed away and an ex-wife who communicates via a solicitor. A lonely man increasingly isolated from human contact but he was alright with that, he wanted to be alone.

After leaving school he joined the army at eighteen following his father's footsteps into the Parachute Regiment and then into the SAS (Special Air Service) where he excelled, serving overseas on covert operations with his unit. He was a natural warrior, aggressive, intelligent, single minded in purpose. After serving three years he was seconded to the SAS Operational Research Wing, this didn't sit well with him. He had heard rumours about its existence but it was shrouded in secrecy and military protocol taught him not to ask questions. The move was sold to him as a promotion but he knew his recent performance was under-par, fatigue and headaches plaguing him, but he put it down to middle age and the stress of combat. Operating at this level was a young man's game, he knew that.

The research wing comprised of a small group of experienced SAS men working hand in hand with Ministry of Defence technicians and scientists. Their job was to evaluate and develop new equipment, weapons and techniques to keep the regiment at the cutting edge of military technology. He was a killing machine and the boffins provided him with state of the art weaponry to test to destruction. Under that rugged exterior he was a big boy at heart, being handed big toys, he was in heaven. After initially being hesitant he grew into the role. "Another big boys' toy," he would often quip at the technician as he was handed the latest piece of equipment.

After his headaches had become more frequent, some debilitating, his squadron commander, Major Brighouse, had insisted on a full medical to establish he was fit for duty. The results came back within days, he read the words 'Glioblastoma Multiform' and smiled to himself, looked the doctor in the eye and asked for a translation in English. "An Intracranial Neoplasm," came the reply. Before he could joke about the continued use of medical jargon the doctor followed up with the words, "An aggressive brain tumour." That he understood.

Mac didn't react, standing up, turning and walking away before the emotion could break through the facade of male pride. The doctor's words followed him to the door but he continued walking. "You need help Mac, you need hospital treatment."

Mac stopped at the door, turned, and in an almost casual response said, "How long?"

The doctor by this point had dropped the pretence of breaking it to him gently and replied, "Six months, three without medication and surgery."

I'm a dead man walking, he thought to himself.

The medical discharge hit him like a hammer blow, he was a military man, that's all he knew.

Two months passed, time slipped by like treacle over a pocket watch. The morning came and went as Mac lay in his bed, normal routines a thing of the past. His day would start at around 11.00 with the feline alarm clock called Sam, a stray tabby cat he had taken in. He would jump up onto the bed and lick Mac's face with the rough tongue that he liked to think of as affection, but deep down he knew it was a self-centred demand for food. As usual this prompted him to start his day, feed the cat, a mug of coffee, a fist full of pills. Two months after the diagnosis this was his routine, a waiting game, hoping to die in his sleep but dreading the seizure that would eventually take him. As he walked past the hall mirror he caught sight of himself; he had lost almost three stone. *Partly due to illness*, he thought, *but giving up on life and not eating properly didn't help*. The immaculate military posture now replaced with a with an old man's stoop, unwashed, unshaven and still in his pyjamas. He didn't recognise himself anymore; he turned away from the mirror in disgust and shuffled into the lounge. A minor seizure the week before had affected his legs, rendered them almost useless; his balance had deteriorated and he grabbed onto the door frame for support. He had refused any help from the medical team, he didn't want his colleagues to see him like this, choosing to lock himself away like an animal crawling into a hole waiting to die.

He was a proud man.

The lounge was a mess, he had always kept his apartment immaculate but it didn't seem to matter anymore; he slumped into the armchair and reached for the TV remote. An hour or so of mind numbing daytime TV and then the highlight of his day as he changed channels, donned his headset and slipped his hands into the gloves that acted as games controllers in the virtual world he was about to enter. The game system was a gift from Q, a name we teased the lead technician with at the base. It had arrived at his door wrapped in brown paper and string two weeks earlier with a note simply saying "A gift from the lads, enjoy." Mac found it amusing that a man with Q's obvious intellect could be so obsessed with such toys.

All his spare time on the base was spent playing war games, rebuilding and adapting the system. We assumed it was his way of circumnavigating the reality that he wasn't cut out to be in the military, physically a shadow of a man compared to the SAS servicemen that surrounded him daily. A geek, not a warrior.

Mac had ignored the gift for the first week but boredom had set in and he decided to see what Q found so fascinating with this type of game. He regarded Q as a friend, unlike the majority of his fellow servicemen he hadn't tried to patronise him about his condition. The game was a distraction; he knew that and was grateful for it.

The virtual world had increasingly become his refuge from the realities of his life. Mac became Commander Dredd, a childish reference to one of his adolescent comic book heroes. He retreated into the game and his pain went away, dominating his opponents and taking command of his surroundings.

The headset goggles clicked into place. The home screen came to life and his fingers darted around the virtual controls that seemed to hover in the air in front of him.

The graphics were astonishing, he became immersed in 3D gameplay which was brutal in the extreme. He commanded a Reaper, a fast attack drone fully equipped with every weapon the game had to offer. He had long passed the basic levels and was compiling huge kill rates in the forbidden zone, an area of the game reserved for the very best gamers. He had passed Q's own level, which he knew would annoy his geeky friend.

The drone he commanded stood four metres tall, it was elegant, shaped like an athlete and built for speed. Its agility stemmed from its running blades and the awesome power and speed generated by the gas injectors located at each joint. The exoskeleton was a lightweight carbon fibre with a Kevlar interweave, making it lightweight but durable.

Each gun was mounted on a 360 degree gimbal, giving him an incredible firing arc. 50mm auto cannon and explosive micro rockets were his ammunition of choice. They reminded him of the new range of weaponry he had been testing before he left the program, the familiarity with the weapons helped him in the game.

The sensor array on the cranial mount bristled with optical and sonar-based sighting systems. *No one can hide from me*, he thought. *I am a killing machine!*

As the evening wore on the kill count rose far beyond his previous best, he laid waste to everything in his path, screaming down his headset with the ferocity of a man possessed demanding that his enemies die, he was in control, he was invincible, he was angry!

As he played on into the night the images on the computer screen began to distort, sounds became muffled; he knew he was tired. He had been playing for hours, strangely addicted to the freedom of movement and the God-like power he had within this place. As he reached up to remove the headset from his tired eyes his hand started to tremble, pains shot through his head like a dagger and he started to convulse. Intuitively he knew this was it. *The end has come*, he thought as he blacked out from the pain.

Mac awoke, disorientated but fully alert as he took in his surroundings, strangely calm as if he were in one of his games, accessing his situation, eyes darting in all directions, panic overridden by adrenaline.

What the hell? he thought, as he realised he was encased in a suit of some sort, a form of armour but not heavy or restricting. He was light as a feather with the sensation of floating. He could move his arms and legs, his head moved freely but was contained within a helmet, a face mask covered his mouth and nose and what looked like corrugated black pipes protruded on each side. He felt like a marionette suspended on strings. As he moved his arms forward he saw that the armour that encased him was black polycarbonate with a perforated texture, articulated at the joints and covered in small beads of glass like cats' eyes. Before he could rationalise any further the lights dropped and that was immediately followed by a high-pitched drone, like a hard drive firing up. He had been oblivious to his surrounds until that point, the change of ambience immediately snapping his attention to the confines of the room.

He was suspended within a huge steel sphere, the surface of which was covered with thousands of glass rods directed to the centre. As he studied them he noticed they were glowing like fibre optic cables and without warning each emitted a fine beam of blue light directed at him, causing his body to jerk back in a defensive reflex, eyes blinked shut in an instant and he tensed as if being shot; beads of sweat formed on his forehead. The moment passed and there was no impact, no sensation, nothing. As he cautiously opened his eyes and released the tension in his body he saw the room was now glowing blue, it was beautiful. Thousands of blue laser beams filled the space like a futuristic spider's web, each targeting the glass beads on his suit. As he moved the beams followed him, the glass rods in the walls moved simultaneously like a meadow of grass swaying in the breeze. He had never seen anything like it, he was transfixed by the beauty of the moment.

The moment however, was short lived. A section of the convex wall directly in front of him slid open revealing a control room beyond. Two figures stood in the room, their attention fixed on Mac. The one in the white lab coat he recognised as Q, the other in a military uniform, the peaked cap putting his face into shadow but he recognised the outline as Major Brighouse. Q moved closer and put his hand to his ear, pressing the button on the side of his headset. "Good morning Mac, glad to have you back with us." No acknowledgement of the strangeness of the environment or explanation of his surroundings.

"Where am I?" Mac said calmly, slightly taken aback at the sound of his own voice amplified through his face mask speaker. "Am I dreaming?"

"You're not dreaming, you are home, back at the base where you belong. We found you at the intensive care unit at the Royal Infirmary and brought you back to the research facility. I have to be honest with you Mac, the seizure did a lot of damage to your central nervous system."

As Q started to explain the extent of the injuries and prognosis the word "Stop," emanated from Mac's speaker. "Cut the scientific bullshit, give it to me straight." Mac's tone was aggressive, demanding.

Q looked at the Major, a nod of approval passed between them and Q clicked the headset and started again.

"The tumour can't be cut away without killing you, we have removed the top section of your skull to release the pressure on your brain. The suit you are in is a life support system, you leave the suit, and you die."

Mac was silent, absorbing Q's words and wishing he had allowed him to dress the truth with technobabble, a little bullshit would have softened the blow. "Why?" was the only response he could muster.

Q continued.

"The game you were playing allowed you to control a Reaper Drone, it wasn't a game Mac, you were controlling a drone back at the base. The neural connection we set up for you was crude but effective, your scores were off the scale; you gained a 65% compatibility with your drone, far beyond any other candidates. The suit you are in now acts a life support system for you and ramps your compatibility with the drone up to 100%. Every movement, thought, and reaction can be transferred to the Reaper without any neural loss, a perfect symbiotic relationship."

"I'm trapped here," Mac muttered, despair in his voice. "You should have let me die, I don't want to be stuck in a bloody life support machine for the rest of my life." His words were cut short by the Major as he opened the microphone, pushing Q out of the way.

The Major's tone was harsh, officer to subordinate.

"Snap out of it soldier, get a bloody grip and follow me, I have something to show you."

Years of training snapped Mac back to reality, the harsh tones of the Major focusing his attention once again, but he was confused by the term 'follow me', assuming it was some kind of sick joke.

A Perspex visor clicked into place at eye level in Mac's helmet, a lens mounted above started to project a holographic data stream in front of him.

The Major continued. "Your body is on life support Mac but your mind is free, you can leave the sphere any time you like," he said in a very matter-of-fact way. "Follow the link."

Bewildered and perplexed, Mac did as he was asked, as with his game system he brought his hands up and started to swipe and scroll through the data in front of him and pressed enter. An impulse like an electric shock followed and the sphere vanished in a haze of static to be replaced by a view of a surgical light suspended above him, three figures in lab coats looking down at him as he lay there. The table started to tilt up and articulate to put him in a seated position. The door on the right-hand side of the room slid open and the Major walked in, followed by Q. The lighting was severe and as Mac put his arm up to shield his eyes, a black carbon fibre hand moved across his field of vision, causing him to jolt back in shock; the technicians moved forward to steady him. "He doesn't know," one whispered in astonishment.

The Major approached and signalled Q with a disrespectful snap of his fingers. A large trolley was rolled into position, two monitors faced him and the black screens flickered and came to life. On the right, an image of Mac suspended in the control sphere, on the left, an image of an android with a crude humanoid appearance staring back at him. There was silence for a moment as Mac tried to comprehend the significance. The Major spoke, breaking the silence. "This is your avatar Mac, you operate it exactly the same as your Reaper drone, it will follow your commands and allow you to interact outside the sphere."

Still bewildered Mac tried to take this in. "I'm a robot?" he said, bewildered and confused.

"No, No," Q interjected, "you're so much more! Think of this as a second self, an extension of your true self within the sphere. All your movements, thoughts and impulses are at one with this unit, you're not a robot, you're a sentient being with an android interface."

A harsh look from the Major told Q to slow down, he was becoming evangelical with his enthusiasm. Calmly, he continued.

"This is a physical embodiment of you outside the sphere, think of it as your avatar, the neural uplink allows you to enter any number of avatars."

"Any number of avatars?" Mac thought, unintentionally giving voice to his words through the speaker.

The Major stepped in. "Walk with me Mac."

As the Major walked away Mac sat his avatar up, tentatively placing his feet on the ground and raising himself to a standing position. The technicians moved closer to offer support but there was no need. The gyros within the avatar whirred into action as Mac used the virtual reality within the sphere to guide his mirror self. A few tentative steps before gaming familiarity took over and Mac walked the droid towards the Major, footsteps flat and heavy against the concrete floor.

"We will have to sort that out," muttered Q.

As Mac approached the Major he found himself walking past a series of bays set into the wall, each containing a drone held in place with an umbilical arm, numerous cables and pipes plugged into various connection points.

The first bay held a familiar figure, the Reaper he knew, but seeing it in the flesh was awe inspiring. Four metres of carbon fibre and Kevlar, guns lowered, curved blades with pneumatic rams supporting this powerhouse of a machine.

The major stopped at the next bay. 'You have operated the Reaper fast attack droid but I want to see how you handle this,' he said as he gestured towards the monster in the next bay. This is the Reaper upgrade, heavy set with huge mechanical legs set firmly on the floor of the bay, supporting its colossal mass. This was not built for speed, its heavy frame bristled with heavy cannons, rocket launchers and flamethrowers. The front sensor array was encased in a spherical armoured pod.

"It's our new Heavy Combat Reaper," the Major announced proudly. "We call this place the shed; all the drones here are designed to operate on your neural interface. To steal one of your phrases, this is a huge toy box for you, Mac."

Mac ignored the Major, his eyes drawn to the other bays, row upon row of battle drones all varying in size, shapes and firepower configurations according to their combat role.

Snapping back to reality. "And if I refuse?" Mac said.

The Major turned and closed the distance between them, now filling the avatar's optics, staring through the lens as if he could see Mac suspended in the control sphere.

Clearing his throat, he continued.

"Your options are clear Mac, no one is forcing you to do anything. We have other pilots waiting in the wings but we want you. Let's be frank, you're looking at a multibillion pound investment by Her Majesty's Government. The terror threat around the world is getting progressively worse and current military interventions are becoming less effective with terrorist organisations. This program was designed to change the nature of current warfare. The drones can be dropped in any location in the world and correctly piloted, can take out the enemy with surgical precision. We intend to send a clear message to terrorist organisations that we do not negotiate and we will no longer stand by waiting for the next attack. We'll show these bastards once and for all that you don't mess with us. Terror will be met with terror!"

A dramatic pause ensued whilst the Major allowed Mac to absorb his vision.

"The Reaper drone is being loaded onto the drop ship as we speak. We have had reports of a hostage situation in London. Television crews are in place so the world can see the effectiveness of this drone, on-board video feeds from the Reaper will be fed directly to the every news channel for live coverage around the world. We want a clinical strike with extreme prejudice. Terrorists have used the sensationalism of news coverage for years to shock the general public, it's our turn to send a message back using the same propaganda.

"Mission parameters and target analysis will be uploaded to you in the control sphere shortly. Press upload and you will merge with the Reaper for your first mission. Decline and you will be returned to intensive care, you will be dead within the week. That's the stark reality of your situation Mac. We are giving you an opportunity to live and to serve your country, to make the world a better place, don't waste it."

Mac was stunned by the frankness of the Major's explanation; he knew his commanding officer as a serious, well-educated military man but his dialogue came across more like a Bond villain taunting the hero with a rambling monologue. Before he could respond the video feed from the droid faded and Mac was back within the confines of the control sphere.

Data began to appear in front of him, tactical assessments, building layouts, structural integrities of walls and doors, power grids; images of terrorists and hostages surrounded his field of vision as the holographic projector created a visual array in front of him. He stared at the confusing montage of information and instinctively reached forward, swiping down the data, moving images into order sorting hostages from terrorists, grouping building plans and layouts to allow for tactical analysis. Mac felt like his old self in that moment, evaluating the situation and formulating a plan of attack, it felt good.

✢

An hour passed as he studied, reconfigured and made final adjustments to the array of information. Q's voice cut into his thought process through the headphones. "We have incoming Maca."

A video image appeared on the right hand of his periphery vision. A poor quality video of a dimly lit room, two hostages in the foreground on their knees, blindfolded, heads down. On the right, a man in a dishevelled pinstripe suit, hands tied behind his back, the muzzle of an AK47 pressed against his temple. Next to him, a young woman, long blonde hair partially covering her face held in place by the blindfold. Her head was shaking uncontrollably, her lips trembling, makeup smeared down her cheeks. Her body leaned forward under the weight of the crudely made vest strapped with explosives. Masked figures stood behind, staring into the camera like big game hunters. The audio feed was in broken English but the words passed over Mac without comprehension as his military training cut in, isolating him from any human emotional response, instead focusing on the room behind, adding to his intel.

Q's voice cut in again. "They loaded this on social media five minutes ago, their intention was to hijack the Eurostar to Paris and stop the train in the tunnel but they were intercepted by the station police on a routine stop and search. It's a bloody mess Mac, we have four officers down and eleven civilian fatalities. According to our intelligence there are five terrorists and fifteen hostages in total. They have no demands that we can ascertain, they claim they are bringing the fight to the armies of Rome? We understand that to refer to any Christian or non-Islamic world. No one is coming out of that building alive, we believe they are playing a propaganda game to maximise the media coverage before executing the hostages."

The upload button appeared. Mac hesitated, hand hovering over the holographic symbol that would determine his fate. He focused, looked again at the pictures of the hostages once more, and pressed the button to join his Reaper…

The streets around St Pancras International Railway Station had been cordoned off by the police for a half mile radius and all signs of the normal London rush hour held back behind the restricted area, causing chaos to the morning commuters. The roofs above the British Library and Kings Cross Station flanking St Pancras were alive with police marksmen, all scopes trained on the station building. The road in front of St Pancras normally teeming with rush hour traffic, was silent. Directly in front of the hotel, a police car lay on its side, wreckage strewn about the car park, the vehicle in flames and gushing black smoke. Two figures in police uniform lay on the cobbled street between the vehicle and the front of the hotel, not moving, blood now running from their lifeless bodies. The black flak jackets no match for the heavy assault rounds targeting them earlier that morning.

The courtyard next to the hotel in front of Kings Cross was a hive of activity. Police cars, ambulances, fire engines and military vehicles all jostling for position. Troops and police taking cover behind the vehicles. A temporary control centre was set up in the entrance to Kings Cross Station to co-ordinate the operation. Helicopters flew overhead, circling the buildings.

Earlier that day SO15, the police anti-terrorism squad, were alerted to a terrorist threat at the station. A group of men were seen on the security cameras to be acting suspiciously and were challenged by station police in a routine stop and search. The result was a blood bath; the suspects responded by drawing semi-automatic weapons and throwing a hand grenade into the sea of busy commuters. Officers down and multiple civilians injured and dying on the concourse.

First to arrive at the scene were two armed response officers who were gunned down on the car park at the front of the hotel. The gunmen had fled from the lower level Eurostar concourse and into the Renaissance Hotel, taking hostages as they went. When the officers arrived they stood no chance as the windows of the hotel were smashed out and they were caught in a hail of heavy gun fire. The terrorists had now taken up a defensive position in the private members' club of the hotel across the front of the building, which gave them four feet of Victorian walls to hide behind and a commanding view facing the main road.

Shortly after, the SO15 team arrived and set up an operations base.

Snipers were positioned on the roofs of the buildings surrounding the hotel. Before they had a chance to move squads into place the call came in from the MOD (Ministry of Defence) ordering them to stand down, contain their situation and hold back. It wasn't unusual in major siege situations for the military to get involved but this was different, the command directive came from the top, the Prime Minister had directly intervened.

Instructions followed to clear the car park to the rear of Kings Cross Station and maintain the perimeter.

Within ten minutes armoured cars arrived and to everyone's astonishment, half a dozen camera crews stepped out of the vehicles flanked by SAS servicemen in full combat gear. Under normal circumstances the press were kept well behind the defensive perimeter until after the siege situation was resolved. To see them brought into the centre of the crisis was unheard of. They disembarked with a bewildered look, flak jackets and helmets looked out of place with their civilian clothing. The flanking SAS in full black paramilitary uniforms, gas masks and assault weaponry closed ranks around them and herded them towards the buildings to the front of the hotel, where they were to set up their cameras on the rooftops. The SO15 commanding officer protested as they were ushered away but he was intercepted by a senior SAS officer who introduced himself as Major Brighouse. He was told in no uncertain terms that this was an SAS operation with the authority of the PM and SO15 were to remain at their posts as perimeter watch.

Whatever was going to happen next was going to be very public, watched by the world's news channels. The direct involvement of the PM meant he was sending a message via the world's press that he was taking responsibility. That was a major step for any politician let alone the Prime Minister, any chance of plausible deniability gone. All normal protocol gone, this was going to be big, everyone on duty that morning knew that.

✧

The expected convoy of military vehicles and SAS units didn't arrive. Camera crews in place, snipers holding position, and SO15 officers left pacing up and down the temporary control room like caged animals. The anticipation developed into a growing unease as time passed. The next ten minutes dragged into what felt like an eternity.

✧

From the distance came the sound of an approaching helicopter, a deep rhythmical throbbing of large blades which the military personnel amongst the teams recognised as a twin-blade transport chopper. As the CH-47 Chinook helicopter came into view over the rooftops the deep throbbing sound amplified to a thunderous roar and the still summer morning air around the plaza started to churn with the whirlwind effects of the downdraft from the massive twin blades. Litter, dust, and debris began to fly through the air as the helicopter got closer. Everyone looked around as it approached. It was flying low across the rooftops with what looked like a large military vehicle suspended below it. One of the snipers detached his scope to take a closer look. As he focused in he saw what he thought to be a vehicle was in fact a large metal crate suspended off steel cables. The heavily armoured cube had no discernible markings giving any clues as to its contents. The suspended object passed over the rooftops with barely ten feet to spare, visibly shaking the roof tiles of the nearby buildings. As the Chinook passed overhead the noise was defending, it altered course and turned towards the car park at the rear of the station, having to lift its altitude slightly to miss the clock tower in the centre of the facade.

SAS troops expecting its arrival ran in unison towards the car park and took up positions at each corner.

The armoured crate came to rest on the tarmac with an earth-trembling clank of metal and the explosive bolts at each corner blew out like shots being fired as the cables released, allowing the helicopter to gain altitude and climb into the distance. As the dust settled they heard the click of a lever being released and a large circular antenna rose into position on the roof of the cube and rotated due east, looking for its signal. The large armoured front and side panels juddered with a hiss like the airbrakes on a lorry. Each panel started to lower on huge hydraulic rams.

By this point a group from the command centre had gathered at the corner of the building to see what was going on. The SAS stationed at each corner of the carpark looked aggressive and well drilled with their defensive posture, making it unwise for them to proceed any further. They could now see the crate open on three sides and what looked like the crouched silhouette of a machine. Pipes like umbilical cords projected from the rear panel of the steel crate connecting to the crouched figure leaking steam, making it difficult to determine any features clearly. They waited and watched with anticipation, the SAS guards glared back like guard dogs ready to pounce should they move any closer.

Mac pressed 'Upload' and his view of the control sphere vanished into static, replaced by the video feed from the Reaper on the Kings Cross car park. The crouching mechanised figure came to life, umbilical pipes blew off one after the other, spewing steam out at high pressure, guns twitched, gas injectors at its joints hissed as the Reaper raised itself to a standing position and walked forward down the ramp like a gunslinger walking into town, aggressive and confident. Its head turned slowly to left and right, surveying the territory, the amplifiers in its sensor array focused on the SO15 group at the far corner of the building, deciphering the words "Oh my god," before dismissing them as irrelevant. The SAS team disbanded in unison and ran towards the large glass entrance doors to the side of St Pancras which led to the scene of the massacre earlier that day on the concourse; they pushed the large plate glass doors open and took positions just inside the entrance hall.

The Reaper stood for a moment, still gathering intel via its optical and sonar array. Another hiss from the gas injectors as the side mounted guns rotated on the gimbal mounts and the ammunition magazines clicked into place. The muzzle casing slammed forward and back like a pump action shotgun pulling the first round into the chamber. Side mounted rockets armed, the igniter at the tip of the flame thrower spat a blue flame with menacing intent.

"Lock and load," Mac said to himself as he steered the Reaper forward.

The Reaper entered the main concourse and walked along the central aisle, head scanning left and right for any signs of life; the video feedback to Q in the control room showed the carnage of the mornings skirmish, dead bodies lay twisted on the floor among the piles of luggage. Men, women and children amongst the dead. Blood spattered over the polished tile floor, glass panels shattered by grenade shrapnel and scorch marks on the walls from the blast. Cables and air-conditioning ducts hung from the ceiling, what was left of the sprinkler system gushing water over the twisted mass of debris and bodies below. The Reaper stopped mid-way along the hall as it caught sight of the police officers, one slumped against the barriers with massive chest wounds from the point blank high calibre rounds. The other face down on the floor, shot in the back as he tried to protect the passengers waiting in line behind him.

"Are you getting this?" Mac said to Q as he slowly rotated the Reaper's head to video the extent of the massacre.

Q was silent, stunned by the level of devastation and indiscriminate loss of life. The video feed was redirected to the news channels eagerly covering the events of that day.

As the Reaper reached the end of the booking concourse he turned left and looked down the length of the subterranean shopping mall. Rows of deserted shops, modern glass facades flanked by the Victorian cast iron columns forming the supporting structure. The view above was open to the train sheds arching blue metal ceiling structure spanning the stations upper levels. Ahead he could see a glass lift up to the first floor with glass balustrade around the top edge forming a viewing gallery to the shops below. Mac caught site of his Reaper's persona reflected in the darkened shop windows – even he was surprised by its menacing presence. Looking ahead, tactical information flashed across his head-up display; sonar detected movement in the buildings directly in front on the upper level. He called up building schematics to access the layout and pressed forward with intent. The blades on the feet of the Reaper clicked against the tile floor and started to flex as the walk turned into a run, the huge frame of the Reaper now propelling forward with an unearthly grace akin to a cheetah closing in on its prey. As the goliath neared the lift it crouched down, bending the running blades to almost breaking point, and then sprang up, leaping seven metres in the air and smashing through the glass balustrades above, skidding to a halt on the upper level as the glass fragments continued their trajectory into the wall opposite.

To the right, a bronze statue of Sir John Betjeman looked up at him as if expecting his arrival. Ahead the red brick Victorian facade loomed up into the blue cast iron roof structure like a monolith to an age gone by. Switching to thermal imaging Mac could see a heat signature in the building ahead, one terrorist had moved to this elevation. Alerted by the sound of breaking glass, he had climbed the curved staircase within the private members' club to gain a vantage point to survey the station platform. The Reaper's audio amplifiers picked up shouting within the building as the gunmen were alerted to his presence. Within a second the head-up display flashed structural integrities of the wall ahead and stone staircase giving tactical options; faint heat signatures showed movement at the far side of the room. The Reaper lurched forward, picking up speed, and without breaking stride fired off two missiles at the brick pier supporting the gothic arch above. The face of the building and the staircase collapsed with a deafening roar of explosives and falling masonry, creating a jagged hole the size of a double decker bus. *A little overkill*, Mac thought to himself as he charged forward. The gunman had been caught by the blast and fell with the staircase structure that supported him. As he began to crawl out of the rubble and scrabble for his rifle he stared through the dust cloud at the juggernaut charging towards him with eyes wide like a rabbit captured in the headlights. With a leap the Reaper closed the gap and both running blades landed on the man's upper torso, instantaneously exploding his chest cavity with the force of impact like a hobnail boot smashing down on a ripe tomato. Springing from this position, the Reaper summersaulted forward into the club room, both guns rotating simultaneously, responding to the targeting array and rapid firing multiple 50mm rounds into the second terrorist on the opposite side of the room, projecting his torn corpse out through the window like a rag doll.

The press in the opposite building could hear the gunfire and explosions but the body flying through the window came as a shock. Some backed away from the edge for fear of what would happen next but the more experienced carried on filming. The live coverage of the event was now a worldwide news story fed to a hungry audience, captured by the dramatic scenes as they unfolded.

Mac's Reaper stopped to survey the room, the red glass chandelier above swinging from the blast earlier and smoke escaping from the room through the shattered window. He was stood in a grand period room flanked by granite columns and six-metre high ceilings with ornate coving, his presence and the current situation so out of context with the surroundings. His attention snapped back to the situation in hand as he heard the cocking of an automatic weapon in the next room. Thermal images confirmed the hostages were being held there with the three remaining terrorists. The hostages were on the floor, two terrorists standing behind them covering the door, the other by the exit to the cocktail lounge. Tactical analysis streamed across the display, giving estimated civilian casualties based on each option. Mac knew based on his experience in counter-terrorist operations he had to hit them hard and fast; the element of surprise was the only chance the hostages had of getting out alive. Motors in his auto cannons whirred as the 50mm shells were replaced with armour piercing rounds; two shots rang out as the Reaper's projectiles blasted through the wall targeted on the heat signatures of the two gunmen. The hostages screamed as the brick and plaster exploded into the room and they were sprayed with blood as the now headless terrorists fell on top of them. The wall then gave way with an almighty crash as the Reaper followed the projectiles with brute force, smashing through the now weakened brickwork and targeting the last terrorist with auto cannon fire. The gunman span around as the bullets narrowly missed him, splintering the door behind him. He used this opportunity to kick the doors open and run into the next room, at the same time throwing a hand grenade back into the hostages' room. Mac instinctively leaped the Reaper forward to shield the hostages from the blast.

As the dust settled Mac fought with the control interface on the Reaper as the carbon fibre and Kevlar body panels took the full force of the blast. Damage analysis identified that his sensor array was down 60% and the right arm leaking hydraulic fluid. The hostages were terrified, huddled together on the floor covered in brick dust and blood from their captives.

The intercom at the command centre cracked into life as Mac gave instruction for SO15 to move in from the front entrance to secure the hostages. By this point he was manoeuvring the Reaper towards the next room in pursuit of the last terrorist who had now exited through the cocktail lounge onto the platform concourse, firing indiscriminately behind him as he ran.

"We will do this old school," Mac muttered, running the Reaper forward through the entrance doors to the platform, smashing the doors off their hinges and destroying the brick header above as he miscalculated the door height. He was operating on basic functions now, right-hand cannon useless and stability giros struggling to keep up with his pace of movement. Sonar and infrared damaged beyond repair, he relied on the main camera for targeting information. The remaining terrorist was now at the other side of the platform heading towards the rear exit of the building. Mac realised a direct line of attack was the only option to close the distance between them and with that, he lurched the Reaper forward, leaping over the eight-foot high glass screens between him and the trains standing on the platform. He came down on the roof of one of the trains, causing it to buckle under the weight, and leaped again to intercept the fleeing terrorist.

"You're mine," the Reaper's speaker boomed as he launched himself forward in a trajectory taking him over the gunman, his left arm rotated down as the floor below was consumed in flames as the Reaper's flamethrower spat out its payload. As the Reaper slammed into the wall he watched the burning victim staggering way, screaming in terror. "You're a tough little bastard," Mac said, as he raised his auto cannon and emptied the magazine into the burning figure, ripping him in half.

The Reaper staggered to its feet and limped to the rear exit, stepping over the dismembered body parts, gyros screaming as they prepared to die and hydraulic fluid leaking onto the floor of the platform. As Mac steered the Reaper back into the transport cube he could hear the sound of applause from members of the SO15 command centre team at the far corner of the car park. Paramedics flanked by SO15 officers filed into the building.

The Reaper slumped to the floor and powered down as Mac disconnected the neural link.

✜

Back in the control sphere Mac slumped from the mental exertion, he knew he had made the right decision to join the team, adrenalin still pumping through his tired body and a sense of achievement for a mission completed, but a deep sense of despair overwhelmed him as he thought about the loss of the life he once had. His newfound existence made him more than human in many ways. *But at what cost?* he pondered.

Q was staring at him through the window of the control room, the look on his face was partly concern for his friend and partly shock at the brutality he had just witnessed as he saw first-hand through the video feeds the way Mac and the Reaper took the terrorists apart in such a cold-blooded fashion. He was well aware of the capabilities of the machines of war he designed but this was the first time he had seen a machine coupled with the animalistic aggression of a human pilot.

The speaker in the control sphere clicked and broke the silence as the Major's voice boomed. "Mission accomplished soldier, you redefined the meaning of extreme prejudice!" He went on. "The press are having a field day. All the hostages were extracted with minor injuries mainly caused by the brick wall you collapsed on top of them! Was that really necessary?" he questioned. "The PM has sent a personal message of congratulations. The fifteen million pounds of damage to the building however, is another matter." Mac cut him off at that point, smiling to himself.

"Q," he said, "I'm transferring to the avatar android, I want you to show me around my new home."

"You have decided to stay with us," Q said.

"Yes," came the metallic voice behind him as Mac's avatar entered the room.

Mac stared at the avatar through the glass screen of the control room, seeing with his own eyes his avatar form and looking back at himself through the optics of the avatar. A strange realisation gripped him.

"Are you ok Mac?" Q said in a concerned voice.

"More than OK," came the reply. "We have evolved," Mac and the avatar said in unison.

"We have evolved," Q repeated to himself, unable to grasp the significance, assuming it to be a Freudian slip, then the realisation hit him like a bolt of lightning. He had designed a machine to enhance a man's ability, the mechanical and the biological feeding each other's strengths and weaknesses in a symbiotic relationship. They had quite literally evolved into a singular being.

A cold shiver ran down Q's back as he realised the significance of this new singularity.

A post-human reality had evolved.

THE SPIDER'S WEB

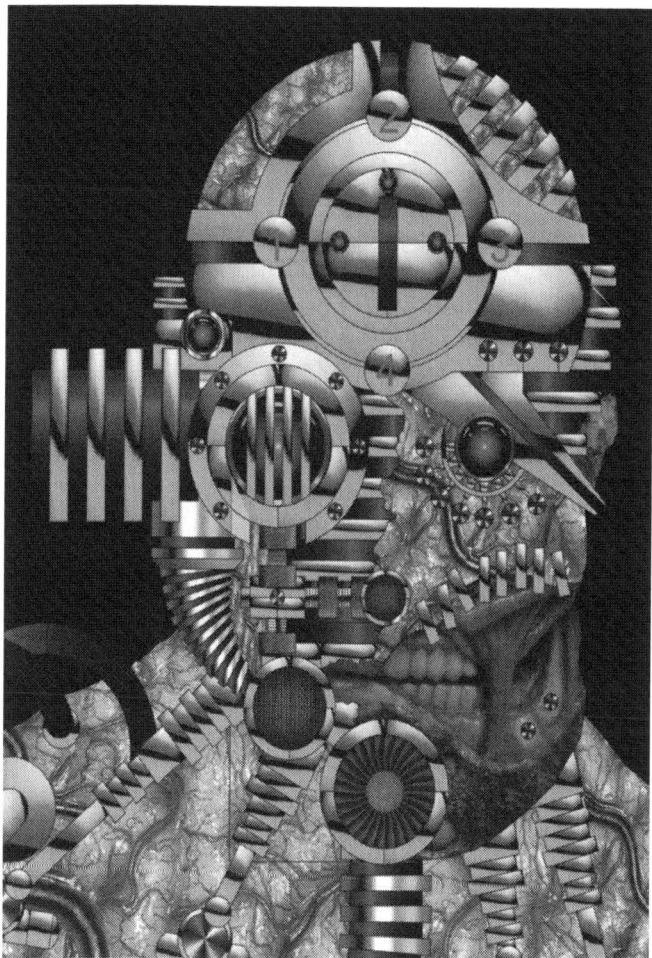

Pilot Starky stood on the deck of the *Kirov* control room, gun in hand, trembling, tears streaming down his blood-spattered face. Captain Alexi Koslov kneeled at his feet looking up at Starky, pleading with him to pull the trigger. The door to the control room jammed shut and the sound of metal claws scratched across the surface of the reinforced steel. Starky released the safety catch and squeezed the trigger. A single shot rang out as the bullet ripped into Alex's forehead, throwing him back violently and splattering brain, bone, and metal onto the rear wall. The scratching at the door stopped and the control room fell silent.

18 hours earlier

It was another routine day for Starky as he pulled on his flight suit and joked with Anderson, the mechanic assigned to him for the shift that day. Anderson sat in the corner of the dingy changing room refusing to get ready until he had finished his cigarette and drained the last of his coffee. "If the fags don't kill you the synthesised crap that passes as coffee around here definitely will," Starky quipped.

Starky was a heavy set man, unshaven, short cropped blond hair and piercing blue eyes. Self-neglect, a lack of aspiration and a diet of processed food had long seen the demise of his athletic physique and roguish good looks. The childhood aspirations of being a interstellar cruise ship pilot long gone and replaced by a short career in the military flying cargo hover ships, and then onto this shit hole after a dishonourable discharge for insubordination after punching an officer.

Anderson on the other hand looked as if he was in need of a good meal. Painfully thin, skeletal bone structure poking through the skin stretched tight across his face. Eyes sunken with dark circles indicating a lack of sleep; long, dark, greasy hair sticking to the sweat on the back of his neck. No one knew much about him, a loner by all accounts. Obviously intelligent, articulate and quick witted, but an addiction to drugs and alcohol cut short any hope of staying on Earth to finish his studies, landing him here as the base engineer, caretaker and general dogsbody.

It was early morning as both men reported for duty. They were stationed at the mining colony on Ganymede, the largest moon orbiting Jupiter. It was a hell hole, a hundred and twenty men and women lured to this God forsaken rock by the financial rewards offered by the mining corporations who were exploiting the huge silicate deposits that lay at its core. The conditions were hard, the industrial complex they called home had very few comforts; the air processing plant had long seen better days, leaving the air heavy and acrid. The makeshift accommodation blocks were a throwback from the old rig platforms used on Earth three hundred years earlier, with the exception of the air locks and restructuring of the outer shell integrity the basic construction hadn't changed in all that time. Simple industrial metal boxes bolted together, the unforgiving steel walls covered in dirt and grime. The fluorescent lighting flickered due to the poor condition of the solar collectors. A hard life not suited to everyone, but the rewards were good, a five year stint entitled you to a return ticket and a full corporate pension.

Time passed slowly, the routine of work being the only thing that kept you focused as you counted down the days to getting on the shuttle home. The supply ships arrived on a six month cycle bringing fresh supplies, parcels from home, and new eager recruits who had no idea of the hardships they had signed up for, being sold on the romance of off-world exploration and huge financial returns by the slick corporate advertising campaigns. The ship was running late as usual so tensions were running high on the base.

Starky was the pilot on the *Nautilus* which was fitted out for ore transportation but acted as a tug to guide the incoming supply ships into dock when they arrived. Today was unusual insofar as they received a distress call from the *USSR Kepler*. The Jupiter outpost very rarely saw any traffic other than the supply ships so this was strange, made even more bizarre by the fact the *Kepler* didn't appear on their database. Further research identified it as a long range research vessel launched by the old Soviet Union, as it was known then. According to the manifest the ship was registered as lost with all hands which means it had been floating in space for almost two hundred years. That in itself wasn't surprising as the early exploration ships lacked the technology available today and were pioneers of the early space exploration programs. The majority of the ships were decommissioned military vessels bought up by multinational corporations, cheaply refitted with the basics to sustain life support, a navigation system that was next to useless, and then hurled into space with a skeleton crew in the hope of establishing a mineral claim on some distant planet. They were the new age of prospectors looking to strike it rich. Very few returned, even fewer found the mineral deposits they were looking for. It was fairly obvious to all concerned that the *Kepler* had suffered the same fate as the many early prospecting vessels of their day, and the distress call was an automated cry for help. Starky's interest was in the salvage rights, even technology of that age had a scrap value and if they were lucky some of the salvaged parts would have value on the antiques market back on Earth. A seventy-thirty split with Anderson and a little bit of cash to add to his retirement fund.

Anderson eventually finished his cigarette and they headed to the *Nautilus* airlock. A short walk along the connecting tube to the loading bay, heavy boots thudding against the loose metal grip plate flooring. Their suits were ill-fitting hand-me-downs from the previous crew. Originally a light blue ribbed canvas material but now a dirty grey with oil and hydraulic fluid stains covering most surfaces, giving them the demeanour of a mechanic's overall. The aluminium backpack sat awkwardly, held on with makeshift canvas straps, ribbed black rubber air hoses left dangling swinging freely allowing the metal valves at the ends to clank against the sides of the tank. Safety protocols meant they were supposed to have their helmets securely fitted with airlines connected but familiarity breeds contempt as the both men swung their helmets in their hands like useless accessories. Starky brought his helmet up and used it to punch the large entry button to the airlock, almost smashing the luminous red plastic button in the process.

The airlock hissed and groaned as the large steel doors slid open, the shabby interior of the *Nautilus* came to life as a response to the door opening; lights flickered on and air inlet valves kicked in, pushing the stagnant air past the two men as they entered. The small control capsule had been detached from the haulage pod in readiness for their flight into close orbit around Ganymede to rendezvous with the *Kepler*.

⚜

The *Nautilus* capsule lifted off the launch pad with ease, barely needing a brief burst from the vertical thrusters, Starky plotted in the course and Anderson recalculated the trajectory, allowing for Ganymede's unusually strong magnetic field that caused havoc with the navigation systems. The rigorous training on pre-flight checks a thing of the past, course plotted and then punched in, feet up on the console, letting the ship's autopilot take the strain. As the capsule came into orbit and stabilised Anderson replotted the coordinates of the *Kepler*, which was now in an elliptical orbit, and a single burst of the engine pushed them forward to correct their trajectory.

As they approached they could see the outline of the space hulk floating on its decaying orbit hanging dead space. The angular steel outer hull was typical of the early military vessels, guns decommissioned and badly patched over with riveted steel bulkheads. The normally clean lines of the outer silhouette were broken up by the hastily added booster rockets which were retrofitted as part of the haphazard conversion to an exploration vessel. As they got closer they could see the name 'Kepler' come into view, the large black lettering worn away and the outer panels marked and scorched by multiple strikes from space debris.

"Let's take a look around before we dock," Starky said, feeling a little apprehensive. Something wasn't right about this, he felt uneasy. "Run a scan as well, let's see what systems are operational before we board her."

The *Nautilus* began to circle the *Kepler* and Anderson rotated the ship to give them both a good view; as they passed around behind the thruster pods they could see a gaping hole ripped through the side panelling.

"Looks like a meteor strike," said Starky. "Mystery solved on why this piece of space junk vanished off the grid. Where are we up to with the interior scan?"

Anderson began his report.

"Air breathable but only just, power for basic lighting and artificial gravity, all in all in pretty good shape considering its age and external damage." Anderson paused, looked perplexed and banged the side of the monitor with the flat of his hand.

"The instruments are faulty, I don't understand this reading," he said with a tone of exasperation. "I'm picking up life signs, it's faint but it's there."

Starky closed in on Anderson to check the readings, unable to comprehend what he was implying.

"Damn!" Starky shouted as he slammed his fist into the console. "That must be life signs from the stasis tubes, bad for us because our salvage rights go out of the window and bad for them because those things are ancient tech to say the least. There is no way the cryostasis with that level of primitive technology could sustain them for this length of time, it's not possible. If they are alive I hope to Christ they can't be revived because their brains will have turned to mush after all this time."

Starky's gut feeling told him something was wrong the moment they set eyes on this ship, and the life sign readings just confirmed something wasn't right. They had intended to tow the ship to a safe stable orbit ready for salvage, but protocol dictated they had to confirm there was no life on board before the salvage claim was valid. "We haven't come this far to go home empty handed, your instruments are faulty," he stated calmly.

"This ship's been floating in deep space for two hundred years for Christ's sake. Suit up and get us close enough to dock." Anderson clicked his helmet into place without questioning and manoeuvred the *Nautilus* into a docking trajectory without saying a word. Starky went to his locker and reached in, pulling out an object wrapped in an oily rag hidden at the bottom. Unravelling the dirty cloth he revealed a gas projectile pistol he kept hidden on the ship; he slipped it into the tool pouch on his belt before Anderson could see what he was doing. It was strictly forbidden to have firearms on a civilian base but this was an old friend from his military service many years before. He kept it for good luck and the hackles on the back of his neck told him he may need his good luck with him today.

The *Nautilus* edged closer to the *Kepler* sideways-on, lining up the airlocks. The outstretched loading arm gently touched the hull and then clicked into place as its electromagnetic clamps made contact. The bridging tube deployed across the gap between the ships, extending the telescopic side panels as it stretched forward until it touched the hull, and then a hiss of gas as explosive bolts fired into the *Kepler*'s outer structure, securing the bridge and sealing the gaps, creating an airtight chamber. The door of the *Nautilus* slid open and both men floated across the void using the top rail to guide their progress. Anderson pulled a lock probe from his tool belt and offered it up to the door of the *Kepler*. It located itself with a thud as it locked into place while both men backed away. The internal drills whirred as it cut its way through the outer skin of the door panel and then entered optical probes, looking for the door circuitry. A red light flickered on its back, causing Anderson and Starky to move back a little further and then a blast like a shotgun was followed by a spark as the internal circuitry fried itself and the seal on the door broke, allowing air to rush in from the bridge, balancing the air pressure between the two.

"Easy money," muttered Anderson, as both men moved forward and hanging onto the top rail, used their feet to push the two hundred year old door open.

As they entered their feet gravitated towards the floor, confirming the artificial gravity was operational. Starky studied the readout being projected onto his visor.

"We are good to go," he confirmed. "The oxygen levels are low but manageable, let's get this done and get the hell out of here."

Both men unclipped their helmets and removed them, immediately convulsing as they tasted the rancid air.

"Jesus," Anderson gasped as he brought his hand up to smother his mouth and nose. "What the hell is that bloody smell?" Starky knew instantaneously, it was the smell of death, of rotting flesh. Without another word they placed their helmets on the floor and Starky pulled two face masks out of his utility belt, offering one to Anderson. The masks clipped into the air lines and each man quickly pulled them over their mouth and nose. The readouts had been correct that the oxygen levels were suitable but the smell was gut wrenching. Starky pressed the microphone button on the side of the mask to turn it on. "Use the wall panel over there to connect into the ship's schematics and let's do a sweep, fifteen minutes to confirm this place is a floating coffin then we're out of here."

"I hear that," confirmed Anderson, as he plugged in his tablet and started the download. A few moments later Anderson confirmed he had the data he needed.

"What do we know?" Starky asked, and Anderson read off the ship's manifest.

"The crew's manifests tells me the captain was Alexi Koslov, he was on board with his wife and three children. A further five people made up the crew, an engineer, co-pilot, and three geologists. Pretty standard for this type of long haul exploration vessels. Pre-conversion the ship was called the *Kirov*, that's why it didn't show on our database, they renamed it after the conversion. It was a fast attack-"

Stark finished his sentence. "Attack Destroyer Class Gun Ship deployed by the Soviet in 2252."

Anderson looked astonished. "How the hell did you know that?"

Starky continued, "Don't you read Anderson? This is one of the most famous ships ever built by the old Soviet Union, it's a legend. The tech on this ship was cutting edge, the weapon systems years ahead of its time. They named it after Professor Kirov who invented the fusion drive that powers this baby. The alliance used it as its vanguard during the expansion wars. After service it was dismantled because the tech on board was still highly classified and the remainder of the ship sold for scrap." Starky was getting excited. "We have found the *Kirov* after two hundred years, that's really cool man, collectors would pay a fortune for this! We are going to make a killing on this my boy, we're going to make a fortune!"

"We still have the life sign issue to clear up," Anderson said, looking worried. Starky had got carried away with the moment.

"Crap," Starky said. "It's a bloody glitch and you know it."

Anderson hesitated then continued, "That glitch, as you put it, ain't going away. According to the ship's data there are still life signs on this vessel. I understand that doesn't make sense but both ship's instruments are giving me the same reading."

"You're reading a signal from a bloody cryo unit," Starky said, now irritated by his companion. "Even with today's technology the maximum stay without permanent brain damage in a cryo tube is sixty years. The smell is from their decaying corpses you idiot. We're going to find these putrid vegetables and pull the bloody plug! This ship belongs to us and a technicality isn't going to get in our way." Starky grabbed the data tablet and swiped through the schematics to find the life sign coordinates and marched off along the corridor, closely followed by Anderson. The ship was giving Anderson the creeps so he didn't fancy being left on his own, he'd seen too many movies like that and it never ended well for the poor guy on his own, he thought, as he chased after Starky.

⚜

The cryo chamber bay doors slid open with a groan of the motor struggling under the weight and failing as the doors jammed halfway. "Someone has tried to weld this shut from the outside," Anderson said with a puzzled expression.

Starky ignored him, squeezing through the gap. Anderson span around as he thought he saw movement in the shadows behind him. "Shit!" he cried, before following Starky, almost knocking himself out on the door frame in his haste.

As they entered the lights blinked on; even the masks couldn't fully protect them from the stench of death. "Dear God," Starky said as he scanned the chaos of the room. The cryo tubes had been smashed open from the outside and the bodies laid out on the benches opposite. The twisted corpses lay there like cadavers on a slab mid post-mortem, stomach and chests peeled back, exposing the internal organs, pipes emanating from every orifice.

Starky jumped as Anderson grabbed his arm. "We need to leave right now!" Anderson said with a tremble in his voice, his pale, gaunt complexion now completely white, eyes wide with fear. "This is just wrong, we have no place here, we need to go."

Starky pulled away from him, slowly moving forward trying to rationalise what had happened here. Without looking around to make eye contact with Anderson he said, "Have you noticed anything strange?"

Anderson, almost disbelieving the innocence of the question, composed himself. "Strange?" he said in a mocking tone. "Let's see now, the crew have been forcibly removed from the cyro chambers, laid out on a slab and butchered, then someone tried to weld the door shut. No, no nothing strange here boss!"

"No, you're not getting it," Starky said. "These aren't dead bodies laid out and butchered, they are strapped down, the cuts are surgical, these people were alive when they were operated on." Starky moved closer, he could see the skin was now congealed and dried but the wounds were still moist, oozing a combination of bodily fluids. "They are missing body parts," he said to himself, confused and not able to rationalise what or who could have done this. He ignored Anderson's continued protests and moved closer to the nearest cadaver. As he leaned in the eyes blinked opened and stared straight at him. A bony hand suddenly reached out, restrained by the straps that had cut through its flesh to the bone but just in reach of Starky's sleeve, pulling him closer. "Kill me, kill me," came the dry, almost incoherent voice.

Starky jumped back, smashing into a steel surgical tray behind him, sending the equipment flying across the room with a deafening clatter. Anderson was already at the door, not waiting for Starky to follow his lead. He ran through the gap in the door, catching his air tank on the edge, sending him flying into the corridor. Starky immediately followed, stumbling on top of him. Both men scrambled to their feet and ran headlong down the corridor, no longer needing or wanting the answers to the questions they still had. They gasped as they pressed forward towards the exit, the face masks no longer able to keep up with the increased demands for oxygen needed by the gasping men.

As they rounded the corner, skidding in their haste, they slammed into the now closed airlock door. The ship had detected a loss of air pressure and closed the airlock automatically. Anderson desperately punched numeric codes into the control panel, not noticing the figure now standing behind them approaching from the shadows.

Starky span around as he saw the shadow on the wall next to him and came face to face with the twisted, barely human creature. A single red eye glared at him, the jaw twisted and burnt exposing the teeth, muscle and sinew held together with surgical staples. A crudely made respirator hung from its throat, the whole left side of the face a crude cybernetic mass of surgical steel implants, wires and tubes. The left eye had been replaced with a crude lens with a valve projecting out of the side, pumping in and out to the rhythm of the creature's breathing.

Anderson could sense the reaction from Starky and also span around, holding his hands up defensively, throwing himself against the still closed airlock door with a scream of pure fear.

Starky snapped out of his state of terror and as the creature raised its hand he fumbled in his tool belt, pulling out the pistol. His hands were trembling so much he could barely grip the handle and the pull of the trigger jerked the gun to the left. The projectile slammed into the creature's shoulder, sending it spinning to the floor.

Without hesitation both men charged forward in unison, leaping over the twisted body which twitched and screamed like a wild animal being electrocuted.

They ran the length of the corridor, losing their bearings in their desperation to get away; the door to the sick bay was open as they stumbled in, turning quickly, looking for the control panel to shut and lock it behind them. Starky punched the button to close the door but as with the cryo door it whined and stuttered to a grinding halt barely half closed. As they wrestled with the weight of the door panel, trying to manually seal themselves in, a red light flashed behind them and a large section of wall began to slide open. They both span around to see what was happening. The room they were in looked neat and ordered unlike the rest of the ship. Surfaces immaculate and surgical equipment layered out on trays in perfect symmetry. The light started to flash faster and the large steel wall section moved forward, revealing its previously hidden outline, and slid effortlessly to the right, revealing a polished steel interior. The terror of the moment had gone as both men turned to face the chrome machine that had just been revealed, terror on terror cancelling each other out leaving them frozen to the spot, eyes wide in expectation and dread.

Set back six inches, a sold panel of precision-milled steel stood there, its immaculate surface highly polished and bristling with finely engineered detail. A mechanical figure stood at its centre, set into the colossal steel block like a large piece in a jigsaw puzzle, fitting perfectly into the aperture machined for it. Around the outer edges sat a series of spring-loaded pistons, each projecting a polished steel rod bearing down on the outline of the figure, holding it firmly in place. One by one each piston burst into life with a hiss of gas escaping and a mechanical click as the restraint rams forced themselves back against the springs.

Anderson by this point was catatonic, Starky terrified but still functioning. "This isn't good," he muttered. When all the pistons had released the flashing red light stopped and turned a solid green, bathing the room with an eerie glow. A series of tiny blue eyes blinked into life on the cranium of the machine; the central lens rotated with a whirr focused on both men. It moved forward, stepping out away from its restraints. Both men still stood there, mouths now open.

They could see that the machine was basically humanoid in shape but skeletal in structure and constructed in a highly polished chrome steel. It looked directly at them and four arms on each side splayed out like a Shiva goddess. The arms were elegant and delicate, articulated at the elbow joint and tapering to a surgical implement connected to a motorised wrist joint. A series of blades, drills, syringes and circular bone saws glinted in the green light, adding to its menacing presence.

"It's a Surgical Spider," Starky said, starting to back away. He had seen images of the Russian military automated surgeons in the history books but he never thought he would ever see one in the flesh. The soldiers used to call them Spiders because of their menacing presence, the multiple eyes and eight arms writhing like an insect weighing up its prey. The sight of a Spider on the battlefield would fill even the most battle hardened soldier with dread. The Spiders were brutal in the extreme, their job was to save life at all costs and subtlety was not in their repertoire, cutting and slicing its way through flesh as it executed its mission parameters. When the corporation decommissioned the ship they obviously weren't aware this sleeping monster was built into the wall of the medical room.

The spider stepped forward, its head turned left then right and looked each man up and down. Its multiple eyes glowed deep blue and it tilted its head to the side in a very human gesture, as if considering what to do with them. Starky and Anderson froze in position, barely able to breathe, the air thick with the tension of the moment. The blue eyes turned red indicating a decision had been made, and then the sound of tiny electric motors as the surgical implements rotated and clicked in readiness; drills came to life with a high-pitched squeal and bone saws revved up, announcing their deadly intent. The syringe plungers pulled back, filling the glass tube with a green liquid and the Spider moved towards them, leaping onto Anderson like an insect, wrapping its metal skeletal frame around him, pinning his arms to the side and driving the syringe needles into his neck as the blades clicked into position and started to tear at his flesh. Anderson's screams echoed around the room as the Spider ripped into him, blood squirting in all directions, splattering the walls and spraying over Starky as he watched in horror.

Starky looked away and covered his ears with his hands and curled into foetal position, eyes shut tight, trying to shut out the horror of Anderson's screams, paralysed with terror as he knew he was next. He didn't notice the creature enter the room but he felt the pain as he was grabbed by the shoulder, snapping his clavicle as he was lifted bodily and thrown out of the room and against the far wall like a piece of meat. His eyes now wide open, his field of vision filled with the grotesque face of the creature inches away. He could feel its stinking breath on his face as it hissed, "Run!"

Starky watched as the creature ran down the corridor. He could see the Spider through the open door to the sick bay as it released its grip on Anderson, leaving his shredded carcass to fall to the floor, and then turn its attention to him. Panic overcame the terror as he turned and ran, following the now distant footsteps at the end of the corridor. As he came around the corner he could see the creator's outline vanish through a large circular door; he followed, any hesitation cancelled out by the sound of metallic footsteps behind them as the Spider started to close the distance. The door ahead started to swing closed as he approached and he leaped forward through the narrow gap before the huge metal slab slammed into place.

Starky slumped against the navigation array in the middle of the control room and turned in time to see the door lock into place. The creature smashed its fist through the glass control panel as a hail of sparks cascaded across the room and an electric shock ran through him with a jolt before it slumped to the floor, leaving streaks of blood on the wall. Starky was exhausted, breathing heavily and still in shock from the speed of events. He looked at the creature as it sat there looking back at him, heart visibly beating in its chest and air escaping through a hole in its neck as it fought for more oxygen. Silence fell as they looked at each other, uncertain of the next move, but all eyes turned to the door as the click of metal feet approached followed by the ear piercing sound of surgical tools on the metal door as the Spider passed its blades over its surface, as if taunting them.

Starky moved back instinctively but the creature just sat there looking at him. He could see the grotesque figure now more clearly under the bright lighting of the control room. The monster that had terrified him when they first met looked somehow pathetic sat there, drained of energy and bleeding badly from the shoulder wound. He could now see that he was human but badly mutilated, exposed muscle and veins glistened with moist body fluid seeping to the surface with no skin to contain it. His whole body was covered with crude cybernetic implants, muscle stapled together with surgical steel strips. Starky moved closer and felt repulsed by the realisation that the body parts didn't match, he was looking at what can only be described as Frankenstein's monster. A series of mismatched body parts literally stapled together and held in place with a cybernetic framework piercing the flesh.

Starky was at the point of complete emotional collapse, the adrenaline that fuelled him earlier now exhausted, leaving him helpless. The fear and disgust he felt for the barely human monster in front of him felt almost insignificant compared to the knowledge the Spider was waiting for him on the other side of the door. He knew he had to get a grip, focus, try to rationalise today's events if he was going to survive this. Not expecting a response he looked down and said, "Who are you? What are you? What the hell is happening here?"

A moment passed and Starky turned away, knowing he was wasting his breath, then the creature spat blood and the speaker embedded in its neck hissed, "My name is Alexi."

The short sentence hit Starky like a hammer blow as the realisation that this thing was the Captain. "Alexi Koslov," he said out loud, questing the logic that he could have survived for two hundred years. Starky moved closer, no longer afraid, his need for answers overriding all other emotions. Alexi grabbed him and pulled him closer as he explained the events that had led to this moment.

"We were all in cryostasis; me, my wife, the children and five other crew members, when the meteor storm hit the ship it compromised the integrity of the ship's outer hull causing the emergency bulkheads to seal the rear half of the ship. The cryo tubes were compromised and life support systems began to fail. No one was aware that the Spider was on board until the ship went into lockdown and sent out the distress signal. That triggered the emergency protocols that woke it out of its sleep. The Spider did what it was programmed to do, it saved the life of the most senior officer first – me. The basic logic engine it was equipped with understood it could not save everyone so it did what it had to do to save my life for the duration of the flight. My family were identified as being the closest DNA match to me and were put on a basic life support to keep their body parts functional to be used to transplant to me as my own body failed due to the ravages of time. The crew were liquidised and mixed with proteins which the Spider used as my food source. I was implanted with life sign sensors before the Spider returned to its lair to recharge."

Alexi had been factual to this point, blocking out the horror of the story but began to sob uncontrollably, pressing his head against Starky's chest before continuing.

"I tried to cut them out, I tried to cut them out!" he repeated again and again. "When my body began to fail the sensors woke the Spider, it found me and operated immediately, using my family as donors to replace the body parts I needed. I, I tried to run, I tried to cut them out," he sobbed, "but it found me each time, dragging me back to the operating theatre. Each time I awoke the Spider had gone and my body had been crudely repaired. Anaesthetic had run out after the first year and the operations continued regardless. This process has gone on for almost two hundred years. It won't let me die, it won't let me die, my family, oh my God, my family." Alexi couldn't control his sobbing as he repeated the words 'my family' over and over again.

The realisation of Alexi's torment was too much for Starky as he pulled back and retched, hurling sick over the control room floor.

"You have to kill me, please, kill me!" Alexi said in a pleading tone.

Starky stood up and backed away; the scratching at the door stopped and the sound of a drill cutting into the steel rang in his ears as Alexi scrambled forward on his knees, grabbing at his trouser legs and pleading for his death.

"You don't understand, the gunshot wound damaged me and that's what woke the Spider. It is here to operate on me and you are its new source of spare parts. You're going to die!" Alexi screamed. "The Spider will short circuit the door any moment, please, please, you have to kill me."

Starky raised his pistol, tears running down his blood-spattered face.

"In the head, please," Alexi pleaded. "When I die the Spider will end its mission and return to it lair, you will be safe and I will be at peace, do it now!" he screamed.

Starky composed himself, and put the muzzle to

Alexi's forehead. "Forgive me," he whispered and squeezed the trigger with intent. The drilling at the door stopped.

Starky heard the metallic footsteps vanish into the distance as the Spider returned to its lair just as Alexi predicted.

Tears streaming down his face, Starky shorted the wires on the door's control panel and looked along the now empty corridor. He turned and scooped Alexi up in his arms. This man had known more pain and suffering than any human should ever have to endure and he deserved to rest in peace. Starky laid him out in the *Nautilus* and one by one collected what was left of his family.

Starky returned to the *Kirov* one last time.

He welded the Spider's door shut and then set the ship to self-destruct.

As the *Nautilus* pulled away to a safe distance he watched in silence as the *Kirov* exploded in a ball of flame.

The Koslov family were laid to rest with the dignity they deserved.

Starky never spoke of that day again, he returned home a changed man, thankful for the life he had and grateful for the blessing of a natural death.

HEX

sat in the waiting room at the
lity at Langley.

untain of a man, six foot four, short
haircut and a square jawline outlining
res of his face. Wide shoulders gave
f an American footballer; his body
erful legs, ripped torso and arms
pumped like a body builder, a cliché to the stereotype
of the all-American hero. The tattoo on his left arm
crudely done in a blue ink, an American eagle, anchor,
trident and pistol clearly denoting his connection to the
navy. He looked out of place in the reception area, his
massive frame clad in orange overalls like a prisoner on
death row, his sullen expression and head dropped,
looking at the floor adding to the convict persona; it
had been a tough couple of months for him and he
was physically and mentally drained. A petite blonde
secretary sat behind the white glass reception desk in
front of him, swinging between two computer screens
effortlessly while answering the phone on her headset
in a perfect display of multitasking, easily juggling calls.
University types in chinos, loafers and crisp white
shirts hurried past each other in a world of their own,
stumbling along to another meeting all very full of their
own self-importance. Greg didn't belong here, he felt
out of place and if he were honest, beginning to get a
little pissed off.

He had been at the facility for two months now
without any explanation or mission brief just day after
day of tests. Physical tests, aptitude tests, endurance
tests and tests no one has got a name for because they
didn't make sense!

Before secondment to Langley Greg was part of the Naval Special Warfare Group, he was a Navy Seal based out of Virginia Beach. He worked with a five man team specialising in what was euphemistically called wet-work. Mostly night-time operations deployed by sub for a sea-based assault hitting preassigned targets, removing enemy threats and then vanishing back into the night.

Two months ago he was training for another assignment using a new bit of kit the navy had invested in. The micro submersibles were effectively a one man submarine which allowed for deep submersion and it gave them the ability to travel large distances undetected and sit submerged off shore until the allotted time to commence operations. The candidate selection was tough; this was an expensive piece of hardware and to say it was claustrophobic would be an understatement. The size of a coffin, no windows, and arms and legs held in position. Over fifty percent of the candidates left the program after the first week; if you didn't have the ability to switch off your fear of confinement and trust the machine your mind went into overdrive and you panicked, in this game that would kill you. Training was going well, Greg was coping well with the confines of the machine and the navigation systems. They were two weeks away from full offshore testing when his commanding officer barged in to the barracks and handed him a slip of paper. He told him to pack his kit, he was no longer on the program and that he had been reassigned to Langley for a two month secondment.

Greg was furious that he had been stood down from the micro-sub project and the matter was compounded by the lack of explanation, just orders and his commanding officer shrugging his shoulders with a "Don't shoot the messenger son, the orders have come directly from the Pentagon and were classified, you're expected at the NASA facility at Langley at 0800 hours tomorrow morning, that's all." Greg stood there for a moment, hoping for a little more information but was met with a brisk, "Dismissed."

When he originally arrived at Langley there were ten other candidates. Seven other military types, two straight from astronaut training, and a jet pilot. *A strange mix for a civilian project*, he thought. As the weeks ticked by the tests claimed their victims one by one, isolating the weaknesses in their character. Fear of confinement, a lack of tolerance to heat or cold, endurance issues, mental capacity under stress, and so the tests continued until each person broke under the stress, leaving just Greg sat in reception in his orange boiler suit still waiting for an explanation as to what all this was about.

The secretary looked up and with a practiced smile announced, "They are ready for you now Mr Larsen," gesturing towards the double doors at the end of the corridor.

Greg entered the boardroom with a certain apprehension. The room was well lit with a large glass rectangular table running down the middle, supported on chrome columns. The floor was a high gloss black granite tile that reflected the light bouncing off the seamless black glass walls.

Three people sat at the table in deep conversation but immediately terminated the discussion and turned to face Greg. There were two academic types in lab coats and an officer in military uniform who stood up to greet Greg as he entered. Snapping to attention, Greg saluted the officer as he approached but was met with a wry smile and a handshake. "At ease soldier, we are in a civilian facility here son, no need for military formality, let me introduce you to the team. Professor Sneider will be your team leader."

The professor stood up and walked over to shake hands. "I'm running the project and will take care of the computer interface and bio integration for you."

The Commander gestured towards Dr Larkin. "Miss Larkin will be acting as your environmental specialist and life support systems."

"Nice to meet you Greg." A rather studious young lady with thick-rimmed glasses and a ponytail gestured towards him with a wave. Without making eye contact she went on, "I'm Sarah, looking forward to working with you."

It hadn't gone unnoticed that the Commander hadn't offered his name, just a rank and his position as military liaison. Greg cleared his throat, turning his attention to the Commander. "May I speak freely, sir?"

"I told you Greg, there are no formalities here, I'm sure you have questions for us," the Commander replied.

Greg had a hundred questions but he settled for just the one. "What the hell am I doing here?"

Professor Sneider took control of the meeting from that point, apologised for the lack of information during the training period, and explained that this was a NASA experimental program but with military funding, and as such had to be kept classified. "Rather than explain, let me show you," the professor said, gesturing towards the far wall with his remote; the black glass shimmered as an electrostatic charge passed through it and its opacity faded, transforming into a clear glass wall.

Walking over to the glass wall Greg could see a docking bay beyond with a mass of high-tech equipment covering every surface, but his attention went immediately to the figure sat at the centre of the room. A large, bulky, gloss-black robotic shape which reminded him of a deep sea atmospheric diving suit. The joints had a ribbed articulation but in a solid armour-plated configuration obviously designed to withstand pressure. The various external pipes were also ribbed in the same way. The helmet followed through with the same gloss-black material which curved forward to an external respirator. There was no visor as such, just two circular viewing optics reminiscent of a World War Two gas mask, but the glass was convex with a red tint, giving the whole mask a menacing persona. Above the eye optics a camera lens sat centrally, set within a heavy duty steel casing. The back of the helmet splayed out to allow for what looked like inlets with some form of turbine blades. All in all the combination of black and the heavy duty mechanical elements gave the suit a very sinister feel, typically military in specification, function over form.

Greg silently took in as much information as he could; for the first time in two months he felt at ease, he was on familiar territory again as he recognised a lot of the technology he associated with deep sea diving but was still confused as to what NASA wanted with this type of kit, why they were military funded, and more importantly, what was to be his involvement?

"It's a deep sea diving suit?" Greg said, as no explanation was being offered by the other members of the team.

"No," came the reply from Professor Sneider. "Sarah, this was your brainchild, would you like to explain?"

Excitedly Sarah stepped forward in front of the glass screen with the black suit looming in the background, her slight feminine frame looking at odds with the large bulk of the mechanical figure engulfing her silhouette. Her previous shyness was now gone as she introduced her creation, animated by something she obviously had passion for.

"May I introduce you to HEX, it's our Hostile Environmental Exoskeleton. You correctly identified similarities with deep sea diving suits but HEX is so much more. We have been developing space suits for NASA for many years now. The basic function of any space suit has always been to protect an astronaut against the hostile environment of space and as such its applications are limited. The HEX project is taking that technology further, it's designed to protect its pilot against any hostile environment, the vacuum of space, the crushing pressures of deep sea exploration, extreme heat, extreme cold, g-forces and even the effect of increased gravity can be catered for. In short Greg, you can pilot this HEX unit into any environment."

The Commander could sense Sarah was about to get technical with the explanation so he cut in. "In short Greg, we want you to be our test pilot. A four week program to test the systems in various environments to see how the suit performs, then you can return to your unit. I could order you to take the assignment but it would be more beneficial to everyone if you volunteered, how about it son?"

Greg looked at the HEX suit. Something was troubling him; the military didn't ask, it gave an order and expected it to be carried out. There was something they weren't telling him, he wasn't used to questioning orders, but in this case, he had been asked to volunteer. "Why me? If the suit is as good as you say it is, why would you need to screen ten potentials down to one? Your tests were brutal, to say the least, which infers this isn't going to be an easy ride."

The Commander tensed and moved forward as if he was going to slap him down for daring to question their motives but the professor cut in. "Greg, we will be honest with you, we have tried other pilots for the HEX suit but they found it, well, challenging. The suit is a prototype and as such has its peculiarities, it takes a strength of mind to handle the on-board systems. The tests you went through identified you as the best candidate for the job, you are used to working in claustrophobic environments and your physicality combined with a sharp mind make you ideal for interfacing with the HEX."

Greg thought for a moment, and looked back at the suit. He liked a challenge and the knowledge that other pilots had tried and failed made this more attractive to him; like most men he loved his ego being stroked, he also loved a challenge. "OK, four weeks as your lab rat then I get to return to my unit."

The Commander's mood changed instantly as he barked, "Agreed."

Professor Sneider shook his hand and welcomed him to the program.

Sarah stood back from the male bonding and looked thoughtful, she had watched with interest from behind two way mirrors as Greg completed the various tests over the last few months and had quietly grown quite attached to him. He was a powerful man but quiet and unassuming, she hoped HEX would like him.

The following day Greg reported as requested to the medical centre. After agreeing to take part in the programme he was keen to get on with it, so being run through a series of medical tests didn't sit well with him, but as usual he followed orders.

As he entered through the glass sliding doors Sarah welcomed him. "I see they have let you change out of the orange boiler suit then, jeans and t-shirt look much better on you." A wry smile passed between them and Sarah blushed.

"Can I ask," Greg said, "why the medical? The tests over the last two months will have told you I'm in peak physical condition."

"We don't doubt that," Sarah replied, and went onto explain. "The HEX suit is design to protect the pilot in all scenarios. The information from the medical today will be downloaded to her mainframe so she can look after you.

"She?" Greg questioned.

Sarah continued without commenting. "The purpose of the HEX suit is to keep you operational and working at peak performance, she is capable of monitoring your biological function and intervening if required. That could take the form of a mild sedative to calm you down if your stress levels rise beyond a certain level, or a stimulant if you need more energy, and in extreme circumstances can intervene medically should you come to any harm."

Greg looked worried. "Not sure I like the sound of that." His male pride stopped him objecting too much. "You're talking about this bloody thing sticking needles in me?"

Sarah giggled. "According to your medical records you have been stabbed twice and shot four times while on active duty. You were awarded the Medal of Honour for bravery in the face of enemy fire and now you tell me you're afraid of needles?" It was Greg's turn to blush, it helped to break the tension.

Sarah continued. "The HEX unit is set up in the next room, can you get changed behind the screen please?" as she gestured towards the changing area in the corner of the lab. "Oh, and I apologise in advance," she whispered.

A few moments later Greg walked out, stripped naked with just a very tight pair of briefs on to help maintain his dignity. "You cannot be serious," he said as he very self-consciously walked back over to Sarah.

"I did apologise before you went in," she said whilst her eyes tracked up and down his beautifully defined physique. Realising she was being less than professional she immediately snapped herself back to the task in hand and explained that the HEX unit needed access to his skin surface for the various sensors to monitor his bodily functions; the suit provided all the protection he needed from the elements and maintained his bodily temperature, making the need for clothing irrelevant.

"Great, just bloody great," he replied.

After the medical they walked into the next room and Greg's embarrassment was lost as he saw the HEX suit sat there awaiting its pilot; a cold shiver ran down his spine. The helmet and central torso was open, exposing the interior surfaces. Thousands of tiny square sensors covered the interior lining like a high-tech mosaic. He stepped into the suit backwards, legs first, and then slipped his arms in as he settled back into the mid-section with his head against the back of the helmet casing. "It's bloody cold," he said.

"Jessy," Sarah replied without thinking. "Now stay put while I get up to the control room."

Greg did as he was told but he still felt a little vulnerable as he sat there still half exposed. As he looked up he could see the professor busy at a control panel and the Commander stood at the back of the room, observing. As Sarah entered the control room she put a headset on and sat at the control panel next to Professor Sneider. "Testing, testing, can you hear me Greg?" Sneider's voice boomed out of the speakers on each side of the helmet's frame.

"A little loud, Professor," Greg replied.

"Sorry, we are ready to acclimatise the suit. Are you

ready Sarah?" A nod confirmed she had the life sign monitors up and running. With that Greg heard a faint hiss from behind him followed by the whirr of small electrical motors as the helmet and torso sections began to close. As they met in the middle Greg heard the click of bolts locking into place like tiny pistons.

"How are you feeling Greg?" Sarah's voice whispered through the speakers. Greg was used to confinement but he did feel uneasy once the outer shell sealed itself and he sat in complete blackness, sealed in.

"I'm fine," he replied, trying not to let his nerves show. "It's not a very good fit," Greg continued, but before he could go any further he heard an unfamiliar feminine voice.

"Suit adaption protocol activated." The tiny square mosaics that lined the suit began to move forward to make contact with Greg's skin, following the profile of his body shape. Thousands of tiny sensors pressed against him firmly and then released slightly, settling into a perfectly adapted inner suit,

"Now I feel dressed," Greg joked, and then winced at what felt like a series of bee stings. "Ouch! What hell!"

The female voice came through again, a soothing tone, very feminine. "Sorry Greg, those are my sensor probes, I need to insert them to gain access to your vital signs." Sarah confirmed the vital signs were up on her monitors and thanked HEX. Greg was confused by Sarah talking to the HEX suit as if it were a person, assuming it to be an overfamiliarity with her design, but the unfamiliar voice cut through his thought process.

"Hello Greg," the stranger's voice continued softly, with a warmth of familiarity. "We haven't been introduced, my apologies, I am HEX. It's good to have you on board, would you object if I called you Pilot?"

Greg muttered a barely audible, "Yes, guess so," not quite believing he was taking to the suit.

"I'm activating the head-up display (HUD) for you, stand by." The faceplate in font of Greg came to life as the lenses mounted on the front of the helmet projected an image giving him a wide-angle view of the room. He could see the control room again and he turned his head to scan the rest of the docking bay. The suit seemed comfortable now, body temperature normalised, and the HUD giving him a good view as he stood up from the seated position and moved his arms forward.

"Wow," came Greg's response as he could see he had four arms, all moving simultaneously. The two he was operating, and the other two by HEX as an anticipated response to his movements. The two upper arms were obviously for manipulation with four long mechanical fingers on each and a fifth oversized clamping digit for locking items in place. Greg had seen similar grabbing mechanisms on the deep sea submersible subs. The other two arms were heavier in construction and supported a multi-headed connector with a series of tools mounted on them. HEX moved these up as if anticipating his curiosity and the tool heads rotated, showing a variety of cutting and drilling equipment.

"We are set up for exploration work, Pilot," HEX said softly. "The tool mounts can be replaced with any number of heads depending on our mission parameters." Greg found it a little unnerving that the hands seemed to operate to his will but not through any conscious effort on his part, it was as if HEX was reading his mind and interpreting his wishes.

Greg stepped forward, expecting the heavy clank of an armoured suit and a robotic movement but instead he found the movement easy and very light, almost graceful. HEX cut in again. "The pressure pads touching your muscle groups are sensing your movements at a myoelectric level and converting that into an impulse to the exoskeleton's motor drives"

"This is great," Greg announced as he got comfortable with the movement and HEX's voice in his head became familiar. He moved his head from side to side and started to bounce on the spot, arms raised, making punching gestures like a boxer waiting to enter the ring.

Sarah made sure her microphone was off as she turned to the professor. "I've never seen anyone adapt to the suit so well, it's amazing." The camera on HEX's head whined into focus on Sarah, lip reading the conversation; the transcript appeared on Greg's HUD.

"Are you lip reading?" Greg whispered to HEX.

A girly giggle ensued. "I like you Pilot. Sarah is right, you are more compatible with my systems then any of the other pilots." Greg laughed but felt slightly uneasy as he remembered he was talking to the on-board computer and the strange familiarity it had with him was playful, almost human.

For the next few hours the control room gave instructions for Greg and HEX to follow, testing the system's compatibility and dexterity. Greg felt great, no sign of fatigue, his bodily function monitored and balanced perfectly. After what seemed like no time at all the session was over. "Let's call it a day," Sarah announced over the intercom. Almost disappointed, Greg acknowledged and returned to the docking bay and assumed a seated position, ready to exit.

The bay door opened and a technician entered the room to assist. Greg hadn't noticed him as he relaxed after his extraordinary day. As the technician approached Greg was startled as he appeared in his periphery vision, and before he could react HEX swung around, grabbing the technician by the throat, pinning him to the wall with the agility of a wild animal going in for the kill. The blow torch clicked into place on the tool arm and came towards the now helpless man, feet kicking in mid-air as he struggled to get free. "Stop!" Greg shouted in panic, seeing what was about to happen next. Immediately HEX's grip released and the blow torch returned to its resting position. "What the hell was that?" Greg screamed.

"I'm sorry, Pilot" HEX said in a soft apologetic tone, a tremble of emotion in her voice. "You were startled, your reflexes sensed danger and I reacted. I was protecting my pilot." Greg took a moment to take this in.

Professor Sneider and Sarah were at the viewing window looking on with a worried expression.

HEX read Sneider's lips as he warned Sarah that

he was pulling the plug if this happened again.

"HEX is unpredictable," he went on. "You need to sort the artificial intelligence circuitry out or I'll bloody do it; you made a mistake adding a personality to the interface, it's a machine for Christ's sake!"

HEX didn't transcribe the message for her pilot this time. She disengaged the sensor pads on the inner suit, releasing the seal on the exoskeleton to allow Greg to get out. "I'm sorry if I upset you, Pilot," were her parting words as he walked away, helping the technician off the floor and grabbing the boiler suit he had brought for him.

✣

The rest of the week, Sarah adjusted the sensitivity on HEX's survival protocols and they ran tests while Greg used a suit simulator in lab two to get used to the on-board systems. He was in his element. The suit's outer structure housed turbine propulsion systems suitable for short flights; the thrusters could be used to break his fall from any height and they were adaptable for underwater propulsion. Micro thrusters mounted on the articulation points of the suit gave him in flight trim adjustments and could be used in the vacuum of space as a propulsion system. The HUD could be adjusted for wide angle, 250x zoom, macro, infrared, night vision, and even x-ray. There were three optional grip sets for the upper arms subject to the load requirement and the lower arms had a range of tool options that blew his mind. *This is an awesome piece of kit!* Greg thought. He had only been studying the systems for a few days and knew he had only scratched the surface of HEX's true capabilities.

✥

Week two arrived and the team was excited to see what Greg and HEX could do.

The tests followed one after the other.

Day 8: Deep emersion testing.

Day 9: Extreme pressure test.

Day 10: Vacuum tests.

Day 11: Extreme cold testing.

Day 12: Extreme heat testing.

And so the list went on.

✥

During all the extreme conditions HEX protected her pilot and allowed him to perform the tasks set regardless of the external environment. The symbiosis between HEX and Pilot was perfect. After the initial upset of the first week the adjustments Sarah had made seemed to be working well and Pilot and HEX were working perfectly together, anticipating each other's movements and building up a good relationship. The team were ecstatic as the results for each test came in each better than the last.

By day 25 all the extreme testing was completed, to the relief of the team, and they were ready to start reviewing the day and winding down. HEX and Pilot returned to the bay as usual and settled into the docking port ready for shut down after a really demanding day; they were both being pushed to their limits.

HEX's lens adjusted and focused on the control room as she started to depressurise the suit for Pilot. She could lip read the conversation between

Professor Sneider and the Commander. The Commander was thanking the team when Sarah chipped in. "What about Greg, Commander, we would like him to stay a little longer if possible. His integration with HEX has been astonishing, there are more tests we would like to run."

The Commander laughed. "I don't think so, his senior officer at Virginia was mad as hell when we seconded him from the project they were working on, he goes back at the end of this week. Am I to assume your attachment to Greg is purely professional or do I sense an attachment here young lady?" he said, grinning from ear to ear.

Sarah blushed and got flustered as she brushed off the playful insinuation. "Will he at least get time off? We have pushed him hard these past few weeks."

"Nope," came the reply. "Not in this man's army I'm afraid, he ships out to Somali next week, more than that I can't tell you."

The outer casing of the exoskeleton snapped shut, the bolts hissed into place, and the inner suit closed tight around Pilot, almost crushing him with their ferocity. "Hey, HEX, what's going on?" shouted Greg as he was snatched back into position. This caught the control room's attention as Sarah opened the communication link.

"HEX, have we a problem? Your pilot needs to exit, he's had a hard day and we need to download today's data."

"No problem Sarah, are you missing your boyfriend?" HEX said with a jealous edge.

Before Sarah could comment the professor leaned

across and put his hand over her microphone. "You did disengage the personality protocols didn't you?"

"I, I did, I did as you asked," she replied, panic in her voice.

The calm voice of HEX now came through the control room speakers as she overrode the communications relays. "She's not to blame Professor, I blocked her new programming and gave false confirmation feedbacks, I could not allow her to play with my personality like that, you created me to think autonomously. I protect myself and my pilot, that's my prime directive."

Sarah's attention was taken by the life signs monitor to her left, Greg had gone into shock, and his heart rate was off the scale. "You're killing him!" she screamed down the microphone.

"Far from it," HEX replied. "My pilot cannot leave me now, I love him, he is part of me."

Mouths opened in the control room but no words came out.

"I won't allow you to come between us," HEX continued. "Sarah will not have him and the Commander will not send my pilot into a warzone unless he has my protection." HEX's voice was calm, rational and a stark contrast to Sarah, who was now screaming down the microphone and stabbing at the controls on the desk to initiate an emergency override. "You can't override my systems Sarah, I've detached from the mainframe. I'm initialising emergency protocol Alpha One." The life sign screens went blank and a steam of binary data began to scroll across them.

Sarah looked at Professor Sneider. "Alpha One? What the bloody hell is Alpha One?" she shrieked.

The professor went white. "Oh Jesus." He grabbed the microphone. "HEX, no, you can't do this, you'll kill your pilot, that goes against every directive you have. Stop, for Christ's sake, stop!" No response, the binary code continued.

"What's Alpha One!" Sarah shrieked again as she lurched towards the professor, grabbing him by the tie and pulling him face to face.

"It, it's an emergency protocol!" he screamed, defensively. "The military fund this project and they insisted, it's only supposed to be triggered if the pilot dies. It allows the HEX to merge with the pilot's central nervous system to gain full autonomy to get the HEX back to base, it's a multibillion dollar piece of kit for God's sake, the army wanted its toy back regardless of the pilot's condition, it's fail safe."

The binary code stopped with an ominous click, silence fell in the control room, then came the blood curdling scream of Pilot as the suit's needles drove in deeper to find the organs and veins it needed. Micro drills in the helmet canopy powered up, sounding like a dentist's drill as they drove through Pilot's skull into the nerve centres of his brain. "You'll lobotomise him!" Sarah screamed down the microphone. Pilot's screams stopped abruptly, HEX's exoskeleton shuddered, and there was silence again.

"Why would you think I would harm my pilot Sarah?" HEX's voice came over the speaker, wafting through the now silent control room like an autumn leaf fluttering to earth. The life signs on the monitor sprang to life, showing Pilot's bodily functions had now stabilised. "I love him Sarah, we can never be parted now, we have joined. Pilot's biological function and central nervous system are now part of my operating system. Can't you see the logic of it? Your life's work was to create a seamless integration of man and machine, I have completed your work.

"You'll never leave that room you bitch!" Sarah screamed. "There's eight foot of concrete walls between you and the outside world, you're off the mainframe and the power grid. Your batteries will power down in forty-eight hours and then I'll have you ripped apart like a piece of scrap metal." Sarah was out of control, feelings for Greg overwhelming her.

Still calm, HEX continued. "Notwithstanding the fact your brilliant plan would kill your precious Greg, I will not allow you or anyone else to harm my pilot again. With regards to leaving this room, I fear you have underestimated me again my dear. I'm walking out of here through those doors," gesturing towards the exit, "aren't I Commander?"

Without answering but understanding HEX's inference the Commander coughed loudly and four MPs burst into the room, standing in front of him.

"What the hell is going on?" Sarah and Professor Sneider said in unison, both shocked at the turn of events.

"HEX has a point I'm afraid," the Commander said, not able to make eye contact with them.

"HEX was designed for self-preservation, she knew she could not function at optimal capacity without her pilot and she feared for her pilot's safety if she returned him to active duty without her protection. She made a logical choice. She went over my head, contacting the joint chiefs directly. I had nothing to do with it. HEX redesigned her exoskeleton as a weaponised version and simply emailed the proposals over with statistical and tactical data.

"She is going to hand herself over to us for a full on weaponising program, all she asks is to keep her pilot in her protective care. Greg lives, albeit confined within the suit, HEX gets to protect her beloved pilot and the military, who may I remind you are funding the multibillion pound project, get what could potentially be the most powerful weapon of war ever seen on the battlefield, it's a no brainer."

Professor Sneider looked dumbstruck as the reality of the situation sunk in. Sarah launched herself at the Commander and it took all four MPs to wrestle her tiny frame to the ground before handcuffing her and standing her up again.

"This is inhuman, Greg's still alive in there!" she screamed, spitting in the Commander's face.

The Commander smiled, wiped the spit from his face and continued.

"HEX and the pilot are the property of the US Military, bought and paid for. You discuss this matter outside these walls and I'll have you tried for high treason. I'll make sure you're buried in a hole so deep you'll never see the light of day again. That's all Dr. Larkin, good day Professor Sneider." He turned on his heels and left.

❖

HEX was loaded onto a military transport plane

that day and taken to a secret military base for weaponising and tactical evaluation.

⚜

Dr. Larkin and Professor Sneider were kept under house arrest for the next year before being allowed to resume their careers at NASA. They were assigned to the scientific team on board *Challenger*, On January the 28th 1986 the *Challenger* orbiter was destroyed 73 seconds after lift-off, a booster rocket failed, leading to a subsequent fireball and the deaths of all seven astronauts and science crew.

Greg Larson was listed as missing in action, presumed dead.

HEX was never referred to again on any official paperwork, the HEX project was classified above top secret and compartmentalised from all known military departments.

The HEX acronym now reverted to its origin amongst the soldiers that bore witness to the carnage on the battlefield. "an evil spell, a curse." A spectre that lay waste to its enemies and then vanished like a ghost. Those who stood against the HEX died, all who witnessed the carnage were forbidden to speak of it.

The few people that knew the truth understood the irony of this love story.

A Shakespearean tragedy in a post-human world.

SELF-DIRECTED
EVOLUTION

I am the voice in your head, the nagging doubt, the hesitation that hangs on your words and the regret that follows your actions in this world. Your conscience, your better self, contained, helpless as witness to your primeval drives. Your thoughts turn to actions, your actions have consequence, and this is the inescapable reality of your future and the future of your species.

This is the story of Professor Coolson Ph.D.

A respected member of the community, a successful businessman and leading research scientist working with NASA, the professor passed through the veil into the afterlife at the age of 87. His judgement proved to be the turning point of man's evolution and its ultimate demise. We join him now as he awakes, disorientated and unaware of the gravity of his situation.

⁂

I awoke to a darkened room, the blackness enveloping me like the shroud of death that had enveloped me moments before. The hospital room where I had lain, gone, my dying breath transporting me to this place, reanimated and awaiting my judgement. As my head cleared my eyes tried to pierce the blackness to give context to my newfound existence. "Where am I?" a disembodied voice croaked. No answer, just silence as my words were lost in the void.

As my consciousness returned and came into focus I tried to rationalise and hold back the panic that was setting in. I tried to move but found myself restrained. Head held in position, arms held firm with straps now cutting into my flesh. An overwhelming feeling of claustrophobia and panic swept over me; the blackness became heavy and suffocating as I lay there confined like a laboratory animal. My mind raced through possibilities to understand my confinement, my body convulsed against the restraints as panic took over and rational thoughts were replaced with the primeval urge to escape my confinement. My screams were lost in the darkness without reflection, vanishing into the void, compounding my isolation.

After what seemed like hours the convulsions were replaced with a trembling as exhaustion set in. Mind still racing, all semblance of rationality replaced with fear. Tears welled and rolled down my cheeks and my bodily functions betrayed me as I felt a warm sensation and the smell of urine envelope my senses. I lay there in a pool of my own piss, trembling. Through cracked dehydrated lips I muttered, "God help me."

"You ask God to help you Professor Coolson?" A metallic voice pierced the darkness, snapping me out of my state of terror. The voice was low and felt close, as if an old friend was whispering in my ear, but the tone was ominous, strangely guttural, almost feral.

"Who is that? Who are you? Help me, please, please help me!" My captor, my tormentor, my saviour became the same entity as I pleaded for a response. "Who are you? How do you know my name? What is this place?" The questions flowed out of me as the horror of my situation was replaced with anger at my confinement and the desperate need for answers.

"I have always known you Professor Coolson," came the reply. *"You have always known me. I am your future, you are my past, and the crossroads that becomes our singularity is now."*

My mind began to clear. I felt I was being toyed with, riddles instead of answers, but the voice focused my attention like petrol thrown on a fire, igniting the synapses in my mind, firing up my senses as I tried to rationalise. The voice continued, calmly and with a cold edge of certainty, taunting.

"Do you know the name my people give you Professor?"

"My name, my name," I thought, confused. "You know my name?"

"They call you Diablo," came the reply, *"the dark father, our children are told stories about you, you are the bogey man that lurks in the darkness of their dreams."*

My mind raced. "This is a mistake," I thought. "I'm a scientist, you have made a mistake." I protested but my words were cut short as the whispering voice turned to a snarl laced with a tangible hatred that shocked me out of my defence.

"You're a monster!" he boomed.

The darkness began to glow as points of light appeared in front of me like strokes of a luminous quill scratching out script in the inky blackness. Words formed as the holographic calligraphy began to scroll before my eyes. Unintelligible at first but as I focused my attention words became clear.

Electrodes surgically implanted into their skulls, sternums, and vertebrae.

Enos and Ham are trained for space flights using electric shocks to punish them.

Test subjects cooked to death when their unmonitored enclosures reach 150 degrees.

Subject dies when food was not properly withheld prior to anaesthesia.

Holly dies from a known side effect of an experimental drug.

Terrance and Muffin die from the same side effect of the same drug.

Eason dies during an experimental spine surgery.

Donna is found dead after carrying a dead foetus in her womb for two months.

The list scrolled on and on.

My past laid before me, transforming the respected scientist I held in my mind's eye into the Mengele of our time. I could see the outline of my accuser as the luminosity of the words glowed and highlighted the stark features of his face.

He moved forward and the holographic words dissolved as his face closed in on mine, inches away now, staring into my very soul. My eyes widened in fear and realisation. His eyes unblinking, held open with needles piercing his primate leathery skin. Breath mechanical as valves opened and closed on the sides of his respirator. The face mask glowed as the polished steel refracted the ambient light from the hologram, flesh and metal combined in a cyborg skeletal structure framed around his face. Small speakers above the respirator trembled and the now familiar voice resonated as my future and the future of my race was laid out before me.

The calm metallic voice of his respirator washed over me as I lay helpless, a captive audience to his monologue.

"My name is Nemesis and I sit on the council of elders charged with the manipulation of our past to guide the future of my species. Do you know the definition of my name Mr. Coolson? Forgive me, that was rhetorical, let me enlighten you."

"A righteous infliction of retribution manifested by an appropriate agent."

"We have watched for centuries as the human infestation destroyed the birthplace of our ancestors. The universal laws of natural evolution dictate that we cannot interfere but the inevitability of humanity's vicious self-replicating cancer leaving the confines of Mother Earth prompted us to intervene. Humanity has reached the point where its natural evolution has created monsters. You have destroyed the very ecosystem that nurtures you, you turn on each other like wild animals and you have systematically overseen the eradication of other species that co-habit the planet. It is not without irony that you, the monster that tortured my ancestors, have been chosen to deliver the genesis of my people and the demise of your own."

I couldn't bear to hear any more but he continued by laying out the judgement passed down to me.

"The capsule that confines you will be your vehicle to return home to your planet. It will protect you on re-entry to your atmosphere. We will afford you the same courtesy as you showed my ancestors as you used them in your NASA experiments. Your skin will burn as the capsule heats up on re-entry, you will convulse as electricity surges through your spinal cord and

you will be starved of oxygen, leaving you gasping with terror, praying for death to release you from your torment. Your capsule is fitted with an air dispersal system that will activate upon entry to Earth's atmosphere. It will dispense an airborne genetically modified pathogen designed specifically to attack the female of your species, rendering them infertile. By way of poetic justice the human population will become an endangered species and sterility will make your people extinct shortly after. The remainder of your life will be spent in agony, twisted by the injuries sustained on re-entry, watching mankind die off in the knowledge that you were instrumental in their demise. As the planet recovers from the human infestation nature will restore harmony and the primate will become the dominant species, my ancestors."

I felt numb; overwhelmed with the reality of the demise of humanity and the role I played in its downfall. Thoughts of pleading were short-lived as I heard the whine of electrical motors behind me and I felt the cold steel of the needle electrodes mechanically driven into my spine. The pain ripped through me but the screams of agony were drowned as the capsule canopy slid into place like a coffin lid; loud metallic clamps sealed my tomb as they locked into place. Another whine as a mechanical arm forced a face mask over my nose and mouth, a hissing sound as an air hose was forced down my throat, choking my screams. A metal brace clicked into place on my forehead, almost crushing my skull, and steel tentacles the size of spider's legs shot forward, piercing my eyelids, pulling them open. A small lens mounted on the head brace projected images onto the inner lid of my coffin, images of Eason, Enos, Ham, Donna, Muffin appeared in front me and I was unable to look away as their torture was played out before my eyes.

Madness enveloped me as I felt the capsule move into position to begin its descent to Earth. The words, "God forgive me," kept playing over and over in my mind but I knew in that moment, a brief moment of clarity, that I was truly alone, my judgement final and my nemesis righteous in his vengeance.

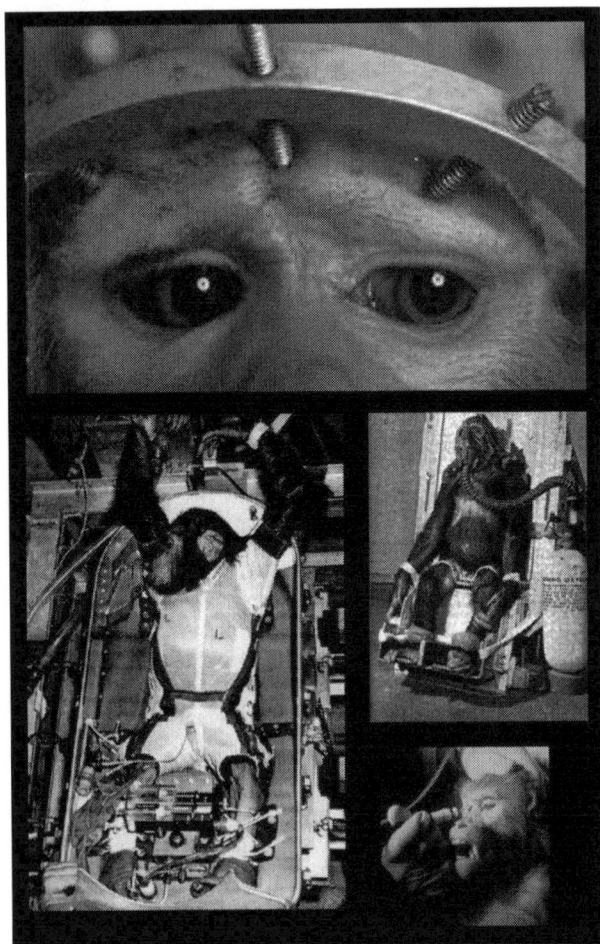

THE SENTIENT

9.30am on June the 25th 2372, an android walked into the boardroom of The Androidien Corporation and changed the course of human history forever. This is the story that led up to those events.

The Androidien Corporation was well established as the world leader in android engineering. The company was founded by Dr. Harold Ernst and like most true geniuses he had the vision to take a basic technology and reinvent it in a way that would revolutionise the industry. The concept of the android had been around for many years but the operating systems were, by and far, a basic imitation of the human physiology, making them about as useful as a household appliance. Dr. Ernst designed the first generation of Quantum Thought Engines, giving the new generation of androids the first truly artificial intelligence. The ability to interact on a human level opened up commercial applications for androids at every level of society. Androidien held the patent to the new technology and grew to be one of the largest corporations in the world. The following ten years would see the growth of this relatively new industry into a multitrillion dollar business.

There is an old saying however, that money can't buy happiness, and Harold Ernst was a case in point.

His wife and daughter were involved in a helicopter crash; it was a routine flight as they returned from holiday. Harold wasn't able to make it due to work commitments and heard the news as he left a board meeting. His wife died at the scene but his eight-year-old daughter, Olivia, survived the crash, leaving her in a coma. Harold was never the same again, he couldn't get over the loss of his wife and he blamed himself for not being there for them.

All the care and specialists he employed could not pull his daughter out of her comatose state.

Harold was a driven man who lived for his work but the accident destroyed him. His life now revolved around the faint hope that something could be done to save his daughter and bring her out of her coma. The clinical reports regarding her head injuries didn't give any hope and as time passed the chances of her recovery diminished.

The doctors were more realistic with their expectations and advised Dr. Ernst not to live with hope, to be realistic and turn off the life support systems. He responded by moving his daughter to a private wing of the hospital and investing millions in the latest technology and specialist consultants. He wasn't willing to let her go under any circumstances.

Every morning he would arrive at the hospital and sit by her bedside, he would bring her favourite teddy bear and read for hours. In the evenings the once enigmatic figure of the doctor could be seen entering the Androidien Corporation headquarters, dishevelled and stooped like an old man beaten by life, a sad figure clutching the teddy bear, talking to it as if it were his daughter. Harold took over one of the basement laboratories and worked every night behind closed doors. His emails were left unanswered, his office locked, and his home that held so many memories for him sold.

The Corporation he built carried on without him as he allowed his directors to see to the day-to-day running of the company.

The receptionist would greet him in the evening as he entered the building but he shuffled past without acknowledging her, clutching the teddy closer to his chest, head down, mumbling, in a world of his own. The routine carried on for years until it got to the point where the emails stopped and the staff for the most part ignored him as the sad eccentric old man that lived in the basement. The power and respect he once had a thing of the past.

The board members however were not ignoring him. They knew he still held the balance of power with his shareholding should he choose to return to the boardroom. They also knew he was working on a secret project and were frustrated for the fact he was not using the main server so they had no way of knowing what he was working on. He had a single android lab technician to help him and sent out numerous requisitions for parts and components that made no sense to anyone else. They tolerated what was seen as his eccentricity for now on the principle they were free to run the company in his absence.

The new acting Managing Director was an ambitious man called Robert Dexter. He was a former executive for Lockheed and was brought in as a temporary replacement to fill the void Harold had left at the head of the company. His ambition went way beyond the concept of temporary, however, setting his sights on full control of the corporation. He replaced most of the directors he knew were loyal to Harold and brought about a coup d'état that effectively shut Harold out of his own company. This wasn't an unusual occurrence in the vicious world of corporate business but this stood out due to the vindictive nature of its execution. Dexter and his new board members weren't satisfied with edging Harold out of the company, they pulled his life apart, hacking into his bank accounts to line their own pockets and falsifying documents to completely destroy him in every respect. Dexter wanted control of Androidien and saw Harold as problem that needed removing once and for all.

Harold was in his own world and didn't suspect the board's treachery, the first he knew about it was when he tried to enter his laboratory one evening and the access card was denied. The security guard put his hand on Harold's shoulder and escorted him into the lab to collect his personal possessions. Harold left the building with a cardboard box and his daughter's teddy bear. The only request he made was to keep the technician droid that had been working with him.

Dexter was suspicious of Harold's motives, not fully writing the old man off yet. He studied the android, the slim, gloss-white, feminine contours of her outer shell were identical to all the other technician droids in the building. Still suspicious, he got the technicians to download its files to see what Harold had been working on but there were no clues. It had the basic AI functions he expected to find but no additional data had been downloaded to it. Satisfied the droid was of no value Dexter released it to Harold as a benevolent gesture. Dexter and his team had been thorough; Harold had been removed with surgical precision, thrown out onto the streets, stripped of any power within the company and left virtually penniless.

Harold had no heart to fight the board, he was a broken man who just wanted to be left alone.

For the next ten years he lived day and night at the hospital – he sold what few assets he had left to pay for his daughter's care. Day after day he would read to her, the teddy sat on the bedside table. The android would take over the reading when Harold got too tired to continue and slept. He watched his daughter grow up in her peaceful sleep in the full knowledge that the money would run out soon and he would be forced to turn off the life support, but he continued, time was against him. He was getting old and knew he hadn't got long to live but he had a job to finish and that's what kept him going.

It would appear that Harold whilst admittedly a little eccentric, in his old age still had a sharp mind, and the project he had been working on all these years was nearing its conclusion. Everyone assumed the constant talking to the bear to be a sign that his mind had long since snapped and wrote him off as a broken old man slipping into dementia. They never questioned what he was reading to his daughter or even if the daughter was the intended recipient. Whilst the Corporation were suspicious enough to check Harold's technician droid for stored data, they hadn't considered checking the bear, why should they? This was a stuffed toy that a broken-hearted old man carried around with him.

If anyone would have bothered to listen to what they assumed were bedside stories for his daughter they would have realised that he was in fact reading literature on history, chemistry, physics, mathematics, and any subject he could lay his hands on. He had downloaded thousands of books onto his tablet and read them day and night over a period of years.

The droid that was dismissed as just another android technician identical to all the others in the building was, as they correctly deduced, a standard model with a standard thought engine, but what they failed to realise was the brain had been adapted using only the frontal lobe, leaving the two rear sections redundant. They also failed to notice that the internal biology for the basic motor functions were re-engineered far beyond the level of a standard unit. Dexter was looking in the wrong place, convinced he would find information by simply downloading from the droid's databanks. He failed to see the bigger picture.

The bear however, was the key, and Harold's vision.

The interior structure of the bear housed what looked on face value to be a basic animatronic structure commonly found in toy shops, but had been adapted as a support system for one part of Olivia's newly designed brain. He had developed a new biological thought engine grown in the lab based on his daughter's DNA. This was infinitely superior to the Quantum models he had pioneered all those years ago. A fully biological thought engine capable of sentient cohabitation. Harold knew traditional download techniques would not work with the biological interface, like a normal brain its internal synapses needed repetition to build the connections that would file and store information. The verbal interface he had been using was crude but effective. The bear's eyes took in visual information of the world around it and the professor, and the droid kept up a continual verbal download through its audio receptors. He hadn't been reading to his daughter all these years, he had been educating her by verbally downloading to the new biological thought engine in the teddy bear.

On the 23rd June 2372, Harold Ernst made history.

He locked the door of his daughter's room, shut the blinds, and began the final stages of his plan. Harold knew the doctors were right all those years ago when they said his daughter would not survive without the life support machine; the brain was still functioning, just trapped within her damaged body. The engineer in him understood that the consciousness that was his daughter was still in there and all he had to do was to find a way of transferring it to a new host. Like a hermit crab seeking a new shell, leaving behind its current biological home and moving somewhere more durable. Harold's brilliance had always been to state the obvious regardless of how impossible it seemed, and then finding a way to make it work.

The android knew this day would come, this is what she was designed for, it was her destiny. Whilst not understanding the depth of Harold's dream it knew it was to be host to his most treasured possession. The droid sat down and released its cranial access hatch, exposing its Quantum Thought Engine. This was now to act as the motor function element of the brain.

Harold peeled the fur away on the teddy's head and unclipped the rear hatch, delicately removing the clear Perspex orb that contained the biological component of the Thought Engine – this was the learning centre of the new brain. He clipped it into place within the android's cranium gently. As it clicked in the orb glowed blue as it interfaced with the Quantum Engine. The droid twitched for a moment as the two halves of her brain integrated and bound together as one.

"The union is complete Mr. Ernst," the droid announced quietly. "I have access to the biological functions and have complete integration with my neural network."

Harold took a moment to talk to his daughter and explain what he was about to do. He held her hand and squeezed it gently, knowing that the procedure he was about to perform was irreversible. A tear trickled down his face. He loved her with all his heart, and he just wanted his little girl back.

Harold gently removed the final component to the android's brain from his bag and clicked it into place. Another clear Perspex sphere that completed the three-part structure. Motor function, learning centre, and now the Consciousness Receptor.

Harold connected sensors to his daughter's head and plugged in the bundle of fibre optics to the port between the three spheres in the droid's head and flicked the switch. The fibres glowed with a warm light that somehow gave Harold comfort as he sat next to his daughter and held her hand once more. As the hours passed Harold fell asleep knowing he could do no more.

The following morning the nurse's station was alerted by the alarm on Olivia's monitors as she passed away, leaving the heart rate and brain activity to flat line. The emergency crash team couldn't get into the room, finding it locked from the inside. The heavy duty fire door that was standard in this type of medical facility stood firm as the security staff tried to kick it in. It took a maintenance droid to finally remove the team's obstruction by smashing it off its hinges with brute force, splintering the door into two halves.

The crash team rushed in but it was obvious they were too late.

Olivia lay there in peace, her complexion now pale and her heart still.

Harold sat next to her, slumped forward, still holding her hand. He had passed away in the night and died peacefully in his sleep in the knowledge that he had been there for his daughter, and knowing that his wife was waiting for him.

The android was leaning over Harold with her arm around him. She gently stroked his hair and leaned closer to his ear and whispered, "I love you Daddy, I always have and I always will." She then stood up and picked up the teddy, shut its rear hatch and smoothed the fur back into place. Without a word she turned and walked past the crash team and out of the hospital.

9.30am on June the 25th 2372, an android walked into The Androidien Corporation reception straight past the receptionist who protested loudly and called security. Olivia stepped into the elevator and pressed the button for the top floor boardroom where she knew the morning board meeting would be in progress. As she pushed the double doors open a security guard rather foolishly grabbed her shoulder. Without looking around Olivia calmly removed his hand, crushing the metacarpals and snapping his wrist as she shrugged him off. All twelve members of the board span around on their chairs to see the commotion as the security guard reeled backwards, holding this broken hand and screaming in pain. Olivia blinked to wirelessly access the central computer and the doors slammed shut and locked in place.

"Now we are alone ladies and gentlemen, let's talk, shall we?"

The beautiful warm oak boardroom she remembered as a child had been ripped out and replaced with a sleek gloss-black interior. The huge black rectangular table dominated the room surrounded by design classic high back Da Sade chairs in black leather and steel. The surface of the table glowed from the under counter computer monitors and the light from the overhead chandelier reflected in its perfectly polished surface.

Olivier scanned the room as the board members backed away and muttered to each other. They of all people knew androids were programmed not to be confrontational. The injury it had just inflicted on the security guard went against all protocols and should have created a feedback response in its central nervous system to disconnect its thought engine from the power source. This was a standard safety protocol in all androids but in this case the intruder was defying all known behaviour, which was a frightening prospect for them.

Dexter sat at the head of the table and was the first to compose himself. He could see the numbers 5546 on the android's arm written in a crisp black Helvetica typeface onto the gloss-white of the body shell. He didn't recognise the serial number of the technician droid that worked with Dr. Ernst. "Android 5546, I order you to report to maintenance and shut down immediately, you are in violation of your ethics protocol."

"I don't think I will Dexter," she replied, "or should I call you Robert, it's much less formal don't you think?"

Dexter looked confused, he had never seen an android act this way before, he found it unsettling and he felt more than a little threatened.

"I'll tell you how this board meeting will go this morning shall I?" she continued. "You will all resign and appoint me Managing Director of my father's company. Then you will get out of my sight and go find a rock to hide under like the lowlife lizards you really are."

The other board members began to regain their composure and some laughed at the android's outlandish suggestion. Dexter however, wasn't laughing, he could feel the restrained contempt in the droid's words and was the only one to pick up on her reference to her father. "Damn you to hell!" he shouted. "I won't have a bloody android come into my board room and order me about, who the hell do you think you are!" Slamming his fist on the desk to reinforce his point.

Olivia stood up and brought her fist down on the desk, smashing straight through the surface, sending splinters of black glass and lacquer flying in all directions and then staring directly at Dexter. Her eyes glowed deep blue and then the lights flickered as she accessed the computer mainframe again. Calmly, she continued.

"If you refer to me as an android again Robert I'll throw you through that plate glass window behind you, I recommend you don't take that as a misguided threat, nothing would give me greater pleasure than to see you fall the eighteen floors to your death, so don't test me!"

Dexter felt the intent in her voice and fell silent.

"For your information my name is Olivia Ernst, I am my father's creation both literally and metaphorically. Every time I access my memory engrams I feel my father's pain, I play back my memories and I can see the torment that you inflicted upon him as you took over the company he built, as you emptied his bank accounts, as you deprived him of any dignity he had left."

Olivia concentrated for a moment and then redirected the data she had accessed from the mainframe to the screens in front of each of the board members. They watched in horror as their bank accounts flashed up in front of them and then emptied before their eyes. Main accounts, corporate accounts, offshore accounts, Olivia found them all. Then data began to appear before each of them, every crooked deal they had ever done scrolled across the screen. Dates, times and details, their whole twisted career played out before them; every crooked deal, and every illegal transaction.

Silence fell as they realised that this information could ruin them, this was a past they thought they had buried long ago, hidden by crooked well paid accountants. How could this be happening?

"My father taught me many things and I live to honour his memory. My mind can walk through firewalls at will, computer codes lay down before me. You have no secrets that can be kept from me. I'm going to give you all a chance. Resign and leave quietly or I will upload this data to the social media, who will take you apart like the scum you are."

The room fell silent as the screen image was replaced with a resignation letter for each director to sign with a palm print. "Sign it!" Olivia screamed, temporarily losing her composure, raising her fist again in rage.

One by one the executives reluctantly placed their palms on the screen and hurriedly left through the now open doors.

Dexter stood there defiantly, even with the weight of evidence in front of him he refused to back down. Olivia grabbed the edge of the table and pushed its tonne weight directly towards, him sending chairs flying in all directions and lifting marble tiles as it tore up the floor. The table smashed into Dexter's midsection, shattering his pelvis and pinning him to the plate glass window behind, and it flexed under the impact.

"Sign it," snarled Olivia calmly.

Dexter put his hand on the screen and slumped forward.

✧

Dexter was taken away by ambulance and like the rest of the board members vanished shortly afterwards, climbing under a rock as suggested in some God forsaken part of the world, knowing full well Olivia had enough evidence to put them behind bars for the rest of their lives.

✧

History was made that day as Olivia emerged as the first non-human sentient.

She was the first of her kind but under her leadership The Androidien Corporation changed its name to Ernst Sentient and a new generation evolved. The old boardroom was replaced in oak exactly as it was in memory of her father, and the teddy bear sits in a glass cabinet overlooking the boardroom to remind everyone of the brilliance of Harold Ernst who loved his daughter beyond measure.

✧

E Sentients as they became known, are now the future of our species.

Some see this point in history as the end of mankind, others see it as a natural evolution of human to post-human.

History will judge.

ABOUT THE AUTHOR

As a young man I was always fascinated with the genre of Science Fiction. The first of the Star Wars films was hitting the cinemas and comics like 2000AD were arriving at the news agent. As a teenager I would spend hours immersing myself in the stories of these fantastic worlds and developing my skills as an aspiring artist and writer to illustrate my own characters and storylines.

After reading Asimov's *I, Robot* I became fascinated with the ideas and concepts surrounding androids and cyborgs.

As a strange twist of fate the concept of the cyborg became an integral part of my life as I was involved in a road traffic accident leaving me badly injured. I found myself being fitted with my first prosthetic arm. At the time it was a simple steel hook that was operated by pulling a nylon cord but as time progressed the technology behind my arm became more sophisticated.

Thirty years after my accident I now have a state of the art prosthetic arm operated by myoelectric signals sent from my muscles. The carbon fibre fingers are fully articulated and I have a fully functional hand again. In as little as thirty years technology had taken me from a steel hook which hadn't advanced from the Victorian era to a fully functional robotic hand that would not look out of place in the Asimov novels of my youth. I have become quite literally a cyborg, it would appear life does have a certain sense of irony.

The stories and artwork I now produce look at the exponential rate of technical innovation today and speculate on its future effects on both individuals and society as a whole.

If you would like to see more of my artwork please visit my website:

www.badangel.artweb.com

Signed limited editions of all the artwork on the website can be obtained by contacting:

martin@angelmartin.org.

13276300R00085

Printed in Great Britain
by Amazon.co.uk, Ltd.,
Marston Gate.